DEATH OF A THOUSAND LASHES

It was an old Oriental torture. It was used when information was desired and the life of the subject was of no importance. It was pain that was unbearable, excruciating. It tore a man's insides out and set him screaming for a quick death.

Now Killmaster lay naked and strapped to a table in the remote hills of Calcutta, a razor inches above his face. The guerrillas wanted information. Nick Carter had it and they didn't care how long it took to get it . . .

Killmaster moves from one lethal trouble spot to another in a hell-hole that becomes a global tinder box!

THE NICK CARTER/KILLMASTER SERIES

NICK CARTER

A Killmaster Spy Chiller

NIGHT OF THE AVENGER

AWARD BOOKS
NEW YORK
TANDEM BOOKS
LONDON

Dedicated to
The Men of the Secret Services
of the
United States of America

Titles are also available at discounts in
quantity lots for industrial or
sales-promotional use. For details
write to Special Projects Division,
Award Books, 235 East 45th Street,
New York, N.Y. 10017.

AWARD BOOKS are published by:
Universal-Award House, Inc., a subsidiary of
Universal Publishing and Distributing Corporation,
235 East Forty-fifth Street, New York, N.Y. 10017

TANDEM BOOKS are published by:
Universal-Tandem Publishing Co. Ltd.,
14 Gloucester Road, London, SW7, England

Manufactured in the United States of America

CHAPTER I

I turned and watched the yellow-robed holy man walk by, his head bowed, his hands folded in prayer. His fragile body had just rammed into me. He bounced off and kept going without looking up, without noticing me or the beggars that sprawled along the sidewalk.

A brown-skinned boy darted from the building ahead of me. He was running, his skinny chest bare, his knobby knees pumping hard. He looked so pathetic, so starved that my hand reached automatically to my pocket. But he brushed against my elbow and was gone before I could hand him the coins.

A second later my attention was caught by an elegantly dressed woman stepping gracefully from the back seat of a Rolls-Royce. The price of her clothes would have fed the hundreds of hungry faces along the street for a month.

I was just getting reacquainted with the startling contrasts of Calcutta when an explosion roared inside the building twenty feet ahead of me. Plate glass windows bulged and burst like over-inflated balloons.

I saw fragments slash into the half-naked bodies of the beggars and rip through the Paris original worn by the woman from the Rolls. I heard screams and grunts of pain, then the invisible fist of the concussion slapped me on the chest and knocked me from my feet.

Smoke spit out behind the bricks that hurtled across the street and smashed the cars parked along the opposite curb. Before I lost consciousness, I saw the upper stories of the building sagging downward. The structure lost shape slowly, like melting wax, as steel beams buckled and boards creaked and splintered. A heavy hail of stones and cement blocks pelted around me.

When something hard hit the back of my head, the pain was excruciating. I remember thinking quite clearly, "I'm dying. And I haven't even started the assignment."

Then blackness came, and I no longer felt the pain.

I awoke to the sound of sirens, those weird English horns that seem to fit the small European-sized police cars better than they did the huge Cadillac ambulance that stopped at the curb only inches from my head.

I felt someone lifting debris from my legs and heard a familiar voice speaking to me from a distance.

"Nick? Is that you?"

The question seemed stupid. But the voice kept

repeating it, and I couldn't answer. My mouth was full of dirt and bits of concrete.

"Are you alive, Nick? Can you hear me?"

Hands hooked under my arms as strong men lifted me gently to a stretcher. I lay flat until they had me in the ambulance, then got up as the old Cadillac raced down Chowringhi Road.

The man who had spoken to me on the street was gone; only the lean-faced Indian attendants rode with me in the ambulance, and I didn't trust either of them.

Not that I was carrying much money. I was more concerned about the weapons sewn inside my suit.

From the window I watched the crowd gathering in the street in front of the smoking rubble of the bombed-out building. A few were pulling bricks from the injured along the sidewalk, but others were pelting a police car with hand-sized missiles. Already the police were popping teargas canisters in the center of the milling crowd, and it looked like a minor Calcutta riot was in the making.

A minute later the Cadillac had passed the crowd, and except for the pain in my head and the grit in my mouth, I felt like a tourist on a guided tour.

An honest guide would have to describe Calcutta as "the world's dirtiest, vilest, most disease-ridden, rottenest city on earth."

For a few blocks, though, Chowringhi Road was a Chamber of Commerce paradise. Museums, government buildings, small hotels, and spacious private homes lined the road on either side, but farther down the street were sights to make a Westerner sick to his stomach.

Calcutta is like most stifling, overcrowded cities—one of the largest in the world. Only the slums are different. A million of the city's residents have no home at all. They live in the streets, on the sidewalks and in the parks and public buildings. During the day they beg and steal to stay alive. Whole families are born, live and die without the crudest roof over their heads, no better off than the rats that fight with them for the garbage.

At night the rows of sleeping bodies resemble corpses lined up for burning after an epidemic. The more fortunate live in slums or *bustees* where the roof is four feet off the ground. The only water supply is the slime in the unspeakably polluted Hooghly River.

I remembered the last time I had been in Calcutta. It was during the monsoon season, and the open sewers flowed through the streets.

So I hadn't looked forward to the trip. I'd come on orders, knowing the city was a cesspool of disease and filth.

Once there had been hope for better times. In 1947, when the British granted independence, the new Congress Party spouted wild promises of a brighter tomorrow through democracy, but since then Calcutta had only slipped even farther into the morass.

In 1971 the people of the city had voted in desperation for the Communists. Even that hope had failed.

The Communists couldn't rule the city either, so the federal government moved in and declared martial law.

It hardly seemed like a city for a man from AXE. But I follow orders, and the message that caught up with me in Nice had been quite specific.

"Get to Calcutta," it said, "with all due speed."

So I pushed an attractive French countess out of bed and caught the first plane east. Now, an hour after landing in Calcutta, I was in an ambulance, nursing my bruises and congratulating myself on being alive.

At the hospital I climbed out on shaky legs and declined the attendants' offers to carry me into the emergency room. Instead, I followed a young nurse with wheat-colored skin and a well-shaped backside down the crowded hall.

After we filled out the usual forms, she escorted me to a private room and told me to wait for the doctor.

An hour later Hawk came in.

I gaped at him. I thought it had been his voice I heard there on the street while I lay half buried under the rubble, but I figured that was delirium. As far as I knew, he was in his private office in the Amalgamated Press and Wire Services building in Washington's Dupont Circle.

He didn't even say "hello." He just frowned, took out one of his cheap cigars and bit off the tip. He lit it with obvious relish.

Lighting a cigar is a ritual with Hawk, and the way

he holds it in his mouth shows what's on his mind. Right now he was either worried or evaluating some new situation.

When he looked up after shaking out the match, he seemed to see me for the first time.

"Are you all right?" he asked.

I coughed up some more of the dirt in my throat and said, "Yes, sir. I'm okay."

He nodded, apparently satisfied.

"You didn't say you'd be in Calcutta," I said.

"A change of plans," he told me. "Flying back from a planning session in Peking. Just stopped by. I'll be going on home in an hour."

Hawk looked at me closely and frowned again.

"You're getting careless," he said suddenly. "I followed you all the way from the airport. I wasn't a block behind you when the bomb went off."

I stared at him. Hawk had been a skilled agent and hadn't lost his touch, but still I should have realized that someone was following me. In my business you don't stay alive for long if you can't tell when you're being tailed.

"Was the bomb meant for me?" I asked.

He said, "No. Probably not. That building was Russian, headquarters for a trade mission. And that's part of the problem."

My boss unwrapped the small package he carried.

The thing he held looked like nothing more than a rusty tin can from the dump. The label was gone and a fuse protruded from one end. It seemed no more sinister than a kid's make-believe bomb.

"This is what you're in Calcutta for," Hawk said. "Homemade bombs."

I laughed. He couldn't be serious. That thing looked like a toy.

"Potassium nitrate," he said. "An old tin can and a fuse. Cost—two rupees."

"Fifteen cents," I figured aloud.

"Right. Pretty cheap, even in a country like India. But it's powerful, strong enough to blow off a man's leg or wreck a building. Maybe more powerful than a hydrogen bomb if you make enough of them and use them for political pressure."

This time it was my turn to frown. He surprised me. Hawk wasn't a man to exaggerate, but he was talking about a homemade bomb like it was a block buster.

"During the past twenty-four hours, three Russian buildings in Calcutta have been ripped by these fifteen-cent wonders. That includes the trade mission and two firms owned by Russians."

"So?" I asked. "Since when does AXE worry about the Russians getting pushed around?"

"Our Red friends are screaming. The police have traced the containers to an American firm, National Can Company."

"But they sell all over the world."

"Doesn't matter. We're catching the pressure. There's talk of reprisals. And there are rumors."

"Rumors?"

"Hints of something big."

"As a result of a couple of fifteen-cent bombs?"

Hawk chewed on his cigar, which had gone out. His face was grim. "Yes, you put enough of them together in the right places. . . ." He shrugged.

He handed me a thin file with a visual apology. "This is all we have so far. It's a State Department problem, so you'll work through our consulate. I think they have a lead for you. Then get in touch with a man named Randy Mir. He's the AXE control agent here. The contact point is in the file." He sighed and seemed unsure of himself. That wasn't like him. "We want to nip this before it gets started. There's a smell to it we don't like."

He paused again, as though he regretted what he had to say. "Find out who makes the bombs and stop them. No restraints."

Inside the file were two messages from Randy Mir, nothing else. I could have gained more information from a newspaper clipping service. I was running blind, and I didn't like it.

I stared at the graying man, expecting more from him.

"You know everything we know, Nick. There's nothing we could hold back on this one," he said. "It must be settled quickly. We don't have time for a thorough recon or even a secondary investigation. So be careful. We have no idea what you might be getting into."

"A snap," I said.

"I wish we had more for you on this one. Randy

Mir says he's got a dog that might help. He's been training a German shepherd for a year to sniff out explosives. It's a long shot, but give it a try. On this one we need everything we've got."

He knocked off the cigar ash and ground it to powder on the floor. "We know little of Russian movements in this area. They do have at least one man here, perhaps more. And the Chinese may be active too."

"My cover?"

Hawk handed me a briefcase, a passport and an airline ticket stub.

"You're Howard Matson. For the past month you've been in the Far East looking for an inexpensive source of potassium nitrate. You manufacture fireworks."

I took the passport and checked it, memorizing where I supposedly was born and lived, where my fictitious business was located. The briefcase was full of fireworks forms, formulas, sales agreements, pens and pads of paper. It would be enough to satisfy a casual inspection.

Hawk fished in his pocket and produced a hotel key. He handed it to me.

"There are clothes in the room. All the personal things you'll need. Good luck."

He strode to the door and left without looking back. I was alone again. Bruised and battered, a stranger in an ugly town, with an assignment that had nearly killed me before I started it.

The doctor who came in spoke in Oxford English

and examined me with the thoroughness of a Mayo Brothers' diagnostic team.

"No broken bones," he said. "No internal injuries."

He immediately lost interest in me. He scribbled out a prescription for a pain killer and disappeared. An hour later I checked out of the hospital and looked for a cab.

Outside in the heat again, I thought about the clothes Hawk had waiting for me at the hotel and hoped he had picked something light and cool. But it wasn't only the heat that made me sweat as I climbed into the cab. It was the assignment. I was going in blind and without a single, solid lead. I didn't like it.

CHAPTER II

Bertrum J. Slocum looked like a movie diplomat. He stood just over six feet tall with silver-gray hair and a carefully clipped mustache. He wore highly polished shoes, an expensive, well-cut suit and studs in the French cuffs of his pin-striped shirt. As he held out his hand, a quick smile flashed across his face and was gone.

"Ah, Mr. Carter. I've been hearing some rather fabulous things about you."

"Matson," I said. "We'd better get in the habit of using my cover name."

"Ah, yes, of course." He motioned for me to sit down in the blue velvet chair beside his polished desk. There wasn't even a telephone on his desk to detract from the brilliant grain pattern under the wax.

"Have you been briefed since leaving France?" he asked.

"Not completely."

"Mmmmm. Well, there have been four more bombings, including the one that just missed you today.

The Russian consul has formally charged the United States with responsibility. They keep sending revised estimates of the cost of reconstruction and a list of the lives lost by their nationals. So far the tab runs to around twenty million dollars."

"That's ridiculous. How can they prove that we...."

"They can't."

"Did we?"

"No, no, of course not. We're as much in the dark as everyone else. Yesterday the Russians issued pistols to each employee in their consulate. They have twenty-six, and I can guess what for. It's a big spy network, that's what it is." He stopped and pushed an envelope across the desk to me. "Washington sent a message for you. It's coded. They also have instructed us to give you all possible cooperation."

Slocum got up and went to the window. After rubbing his hand over his face, he returned. "Carter ... I mean Matson ... we must stop these bombing attacks at once and get the Russians off our necks. This is the first blot on my record. Twenty-seven years with the State Department, and now this."

"I'll do my best, Mr. Slocum. But I do need a few items. Fifty rounds for a standard 9mm Luger pistol, a good, small .25 caliber automatic and two fragmentation grenades."

"Mr. Matson! I'm a diplomat, not a war supply office."

I laughed. "You want me to hold a diplomatic discussion with a terrorist who's throwing a bomb at me? I'll use my methods, you use yours. I'll also need a car and a thousand dollars in rupees, nothing larger than a twenty rupee note."

Slocum considered me for a moment and I could see the disgust in his eyes. I was far beneath him in his personal interpretation of rank. At the moment, though, he needed me.

Without a word he picked up the phone and started issuing orders. While he worked, I opened the envelope he had given me and scanned the neatly typed set of numbers and letters. The message was in a five-pattern dialogical AXE code. I would have preferred to destroy the communiqué immediately, but you don't memorize a five-pattern, so I stuffed it in my pocket.

Slocum handed me a set of car keys and a stack of rupee notes, most of them well worn, which was what I wanted. The car keys had a circle and triangle stamped on them. So I figured they must be for a Mercedes, probably Slocum's personal car. He was making some sacrifices after all.

"Mr. Matson, Washington asks me to remind you that this has the makings of a first-class confrontation between the U.S. and Russia. It seems we are cast as the villain with no way to prove our innocence. If the current scale of bombings is escalated or if any more of the Russian consulate personnel are killed...."

He wiped his brow. Slocum was sweating in his refrigerated office. "Well, we could see a full-scale guerrilla war right here in Calcutta. Americans and

Russians at each others' throats in a neutral country—a frightening prospect."

"If that happens, Mr. Slocum, you won't need me. You'll need the Marines."

Back in my hotel room a half-hour later, I labored over the coded message I had received from the States. The instructions were curt.

"Suggest you meet and maintain contact with Chuni Mehta, daughter of the famous industrialist. Known Indian Agent M4 class, their lowest. Moved up from courier. Seems to work only on part-time basis. May be valuable for help with special Calcutta problems. She is known to be sympathetic to U.S., but do not break cover with her unless necessary."

The message wasn't much, but it helped. At least it gave me one possible ally, and they were mighty scarce in Calcutta since the U.S. government had sided with the Pakistanis in the war with India. I thumbed through the phone book until at last I found the name of a society editor for an English-language newspaper. Posing as a free-lance writer, I got most of the information I wanted.

Chuni Mehta was twenty-two, about five-seven, a high-caste Brahmin. She had gone to school in Switzerland and had a reputation as a jet-setter. She played tennis every day at the Racquette and Cricket Club near Maidan Park.

Meeting her was easier than I'd thought it would be. I simply barged up to the club, where she was thoroughly whipping a washed-out-looking English girl. After ten rupees passed hands, the bartender told me Chuni's favorite drink was a gin fizz, so I took two with me as I went out to the court.

She drilled a sideline shot past her opponent.

"Game," Chuni said, moving toward the net.

"That shot deserves a drink," I said, holding a glass out to her.

A frown creased her forehead, then vanished. I plunged on.

"Some friends in Monte Carlo said I had to look you up if I ever came to Calcutta. So here I am."

"Yes." Her voice was low, pleasant, with a faint British accent and a hint of snobbery. "What friends?"

I smiled. "Sorry, I never repeat names. Just friends."

There was a smile now at the corners of her lips. She was beautiful, with skin a light shade of olive. Her eyes were brown, her hair black and shining, hanging in twin braids halfway down her back.

"I think you're lying, but thank you for the drink," she said. She sipped at it, then handed it to me. "Hold this. If you want to wait until we finish this set . . . we can talk." She laughed. "Talk about those friends of ours in Monte Carlo. I've never been there."

She turned, showing me her rounded rump under the short, white tennis dress. I was glad someone in AXE had suggested I make this contact. She was going to add a little diversion to the assignment.

Chuni served well, a booming drive with good top

spin. She won the last set six to one and came toward me, blotting at the sweat on her forehead.

"Not bad."

She laughed. "Me or the tennis?"

"Both. You're the first Indian girl I've seen who had real legs."

Chuni laughed, taking the drink from me. "I'm a scandal. In Switzerland or London it's considered very chic. But here, legs are for cows and men."

She put the drink down on the bench and turned toward me, the top of her tennis dress accenting her fine breasts. She was aware of the effect. "You're American, correct?"

"Right, and looking for someone to have dinner with. How about it?"

She looked surprised. "Why?"

"You're beautiful, intelligent, sexy. And I'm tired and bored and need a night on the town." I paused. "Pardon me, my name is Howard Matson. I'm from New York City, and I'm here buying fireworks."

"Firecrackers, rockets?"

"Yes."

"Weird." She paused. "Why not? Only, you'd be surprised how dull this town can be. Why not make it dinner at my apartment, about eight?"

"Don't go to any trouble. . . ."

"I'll tell my cook to keep it simple." She laughed at me as she rose. "I'm heading for the showers. I'll see you tonight." She turned and walked toward the clubhouse.

"Hey, I don't even know where you live." I ran to catch her. She stopped.

"Mr. Matson, you found out I was here on the courts. You discovered I've done some traveling and you probably bribed somebody to find out what I drink. I'm sure you won't have any trouble finding where I live. If you can't, I'm afraid you'll miss your dinner." She turned away again and continued toward the showers.

Outside the women's dressing room I saw her stop and speak to an old grim-faced man. The club astrologer, I guessed. From where I stood I could see his library of celestial computations inscribed on birchbark strips, and I wondered if she were asking his advice about me.

His presence reminded me of the two faces of India . . . the modern side that produced sophisticated women like Chuni Mehta and the ancient past that clings to them with tentacles of religion and the occult.

This duplicity would make my assignment more difficult. As I left the club, I decided to talk to the local AXE control agent immediately. Maybe he could help me better understand this culture where some people walked naked through the streets with their bodies coated with ashes while others wore eye shadow and lipstick.

I knew very little about Randy Mir, although I had heard his name before. He was a full-time man, supposedly acting as watch dog, a lookout who kept a safe house for our people who worked or passed through India.

It was nearly four when I approached his shop, a bookstore with the usual beggar outside. It was a woman this time, a widow. I could tell that by the word "rama" that she had tattooed repeatedly in lines of Sanskrit across her face.

"*Hare Krishna, Hare Rama,*" she chanted beneath her shroudlike sari and shawl.

I passed her quickly. For all I knew, she was an agent, too, a lookout for Randy Mir or a counter-agent for the Communists.

I had parked two blocks from the store and had left the Mercedes with an Indian soldier eyeballing it from across the littered street. He stood with a rifle slung across his shoulder, and I gathered from his nod that he intended to watch it.

The sight of his gun made me think of Wilhelmina resting in her holster under my left arm. And there was Hugo too, my long stiletto, strapped securely to my right wrist where I could get to it in a microsecond.

I was ready for Calcutta, but I was still cautious. I walked past the front of the store, checking for a rear entrance and trying to be casual.

Even at four-thirty the street was a blinding glare of heat. The white stones threw the sun back at me from every angle. At the corner I turned off Chowringhi and angled toward the rear of the small bookstall.

I was walking down the narrow street when I felt something had changed. The cadence of the sounds in the street was different. Some element had shifted. I glanced behind me and saw only two ragged little boys, neither over eight. They carried small stones tied to strings which they swung in a curious way, stopping and starting the swing, making up a game as they walked.

I moved on, peering in shops like an idle tourist or a businessman with a few moments to waste in a strange city.

Without knowing why, I felt uncomfortable, hesitant to enter the shop of Randy Mir.

The bookstore was a block behind me now and I stopped, ready to retrace my steps, when I heard a man striding purposefully toward me.

His pace quickened and I whirled instinctively.

I saw the knife first, then the hand that held it.

The Indian swore to himself in Hindi. He had the knife low and ready. A second later I had Hugo in my right hand and was moving to meet the attacker.

The man was good but not an expert. He drove in, stopped, turned and slashed. But I knew what he was going to do. It was as if he had finished only part of his training. I countered, my blade slicing deeply across his wrist. He dropped the knife and tried to run, but I tripped him. Before he could jump up, my foot was on his chest pinning his light body to the stones.

"Who the hell are you?" I asked. He mumbled a

name that meant nothing to me. "Who sent you?"

He shook his head. I repeated the question in English. Still he did not respond. His wrist kept bleeding. I pointed to it, but he only shrugged. Who was he? I had to know. Was he simply trying to rob me or had he tried to kill me on someone's orders.

I laid my blade next to his throat and sliced into the skin so a trickle of blood showed. "Who?" I asked again in Hindi.

His eyes widened in honest fear. He squirmed away. I put more pressure on the knife, seeing it slice a fraction of millimeter deeper. "Who?" I probed again.

"Zakir," he said, yelping with pain. "Zakir sent me."

"Zakir who?"

His breath came in gasps; his eyes widened again as he looked at the blood dripping from his wrist. Then his head tipped to one side as he lost consciousness.

"Damn," I mumbled.

I wanted to know a lot more. Was my cover blown already? Who was this Zakir? He might be nothing more than a cheap hoodlum.

I bent down to shake him awake but had to stop as a colorfully dressed band of Indians turned into the street.

The man in the lead wore the ocher robe and the tinseled headgear of a bridegroom. Tied to him with a symbolic cord of silk was his veiled bride. Behind them came the wedding party, a dozen or more richly robed members of the family.

At the sight of the blood dripping from the dying man on the walk, the party froze. They stared at me, waiting.

I had no choice. It could be five minutes before the man with the knife recovered long enough to talk. By then a large crowd would have gathered. It was not an ideal set-up for interrogating the man.

I wondered if he was alone. Did he have a backup waiting for me in this narrow alley? I walked faster, then sprinted out of the passageway and down another street before I stopped. I was sweating through my new suit as I tried to get my bearings.

I knew the man had been trying to kill me, but why? Because I was Nick Carter, or because I might have a few rupees in my pocket?

When I reached the bookshop, I decided to go in the back way. At the blind alley I paused and checked it out critically. I saw no one, nothing dangerous. I walked up the alley with caution.

If it had been a hit, how had they spotted me so quickly? It could have been the taxi driver. Lay out ten rupees for a reward, and you could buy half the taxi drivers and rickshawallas at the airport. Finding the destination of a tall American would have been easy. There isn't anyplace where money speaks louder than it does in Calcutta.

I moved up to the rear door and tried the knob. It wasn't locked. I entered a room that looked like a warehouse and saw a young woman sitting on a wooden bench. I closed the door gently, smiling at her so she wouldn't scream. To my surprise she smiled back.

She was pretty with light brown skin, sleek, soft dark hair and green eyes that contrasted with her Indian face. Her body was finely formed.

"You must be the American," she said.

"I'm sorry, I didn't mean to break in on you. . . ."

She waved her hand, dismissing it. "My father is not here, but he will return soon. He knows you have arrived in Calcutta. My name is Lily Mir."

At least I had been expected. I breathed a sigh. This part of the operation seemed to be going according to plan.

The girl wore the traditional tight, white blouse and a sari. Her skirt, a rainbow of colors, was cut in the long, full fashion. She rose gracefully from the bench.

"Can I fix you a cup of coffee?"

She led me into a neat, clean and softly scented living room. No one else was there. A low settee fronted one wall. Two doorways opened into other rooms at the left, and straight ahead was another door leading into the bookshop.

From long habit I began a quick scan for listening devices. The girl watched me without question. I could tell her father had trained her in his business.

I didn't expect to find anything, but a safe house is sometimes a sham. And in my business, searching the home of your host is no breach of social etiquette.

There were no bugs in the usual places where a supposedly casual visitor could place one with a glob of putty or glue. And there were none on the table or on the doorjambs, none on the bottoms of the chairs.

I had decided Randy Mir must be better than I thought, when I saw it . . . a thumbtack that was slightly too large. It had been pushed into the wall almost at the floor near the front door.

I pulled it out delicately and looked at the underside. A thin sheet of plastic covered the sub-miniature pickup-and-sending set. It was a new type, but I judged the sending range at not over 200 yards.

Lily came and watched me. I held my finger to my lips and she frowned. Before I could speak, a door opened and a man came into the room. He was forty, small, with a shaved head, large Gandhi-type glasses and a nose that had been broken several times and never put back into shape.

I held out the transmitter in my hand. He glared at it but didn't speak. I showed him where I had found it. The man knocked the bug from my hand and ground it to dust against the floor under his hard leather shoe.

"I had no idea . . . ," he began.

"Where can we talk?"

Randy Mir led me through the back door to the alley, where it was dark now. It took me only a few minutes to learn everything Mir knew about the bombings. He knew nothing more than I did. I was still blind.

"Do you know a man called Zakir?"

Mir nodded. "It is a common name in India. I have four relatives named Zakir. In Calcutta alone there must be thousands. . . ." He shook his head. "The transmitter . . . it is my fault. I thought they did not suspect me, but now they know. I am worthless to you."

"And they know we found one of the bugs. They might have more, so let them listen but to nothing important."

I told him about the man with the knife in the street. He sucked in his breath. "I do not believe the man was trying to rob you. He could have been an assassin. Let me make some inquiries."

Back in the bookshop a few minutes later, I took a good look around. By now they knew the sound of my voice. So I had to play bait for their trap, whoever they were. The bookshop was closed, with metal grilles over the windows, and I stood checking from the front windows, guessing where their spotter would be. The transmitter was short range. From the window I saw a dozen places where men could be planted with receivers. The balconies directly across the street would be ideal.

But who? Russians? Chicoms? The Indians' own intelligence network?

I couldn't recall being spotted so early in an assignment. I felt like a hunter who discovers he's being tracked by a grizzly he hasn't even seen.

Before I had a chance to formulate my thoughts, I saw something move outside. It was quick and surreptitious, like an animal stalking prey.

Down the street another shadow faded toward the bookshop. Then an entire pack materialized, dozens of man-shaped forms with rocks and sticks and homemade spears clutched in their hands.

The first rock hit the metal grille and bounced off. The next one crashed through the small window in the door. Then another shattered the big window in front of me. I jumped back from the showering glass.

"They're after you," Randy Mir shouted from behind me. "They know you're here."

I agreed. Someone was trying to finish the job they had bungled on the street, only this time they would cover it up with a small-sized riot.

I moved away from the window, pulling Lily back with me. Her eyes were wide with terror. When we reached the living room, her father closed and bolted the door behind us.

"We're leaving," I ordered. "You and your daughter . . . out the back door quickly."

He started to protest. I pushed him gently toward the rear. He looked at me, blinked, then nodded and led us into the storage room.

Mir opened the outside door and stepped halfway out. His cry came suddenly as he was propelled back into the room, a three-foot wooden spear protruding from his chest, his soft, serious eyes already deep brown pools of death.

I kicked the door closed and smashed the one light in the room.

We were trapped, cut off from both front and rear. The girl tried to say something, but the whoosh of the fire bomb inside the bookstore blotted it out. We were nailed down, the fire in front and a mob behind us.

CHAPTER III

Before I could move, a small river of burning gasoline flowed under the door from the bookshop. I
jumped over the body of Mir and crouched low
against the wall. As I opened the rear door a few
inches, a bullet smacked into the wood and a dozen
rocks clattered against it. I closed it fast and bolted
it. I peered through a small window to the right of
the door, saw a form rush from a doorway and fired
quickly, dropping the man. Another storm of rocks
and bullets hit the door and smashed the window.

Lily had thrown a rug over the burning gasoline,
smothering the flames, but it wouldn't take long for
the fire in the bookstore to eat through the wooden
door.

I had almost made up my mind to rush out the
back door when another fire bomb hit. The back
door blazed with gasoline. We were sealed inside—
trapped.

"Lily, is there another way out?"

She was crying, almost hysterically, shaking her head. I went to the far side of the room. It was stacked with old files, cardboard boxes, crates. I pulled them down. There had to be some way out. Lily slumped by her father, holding his hand. I jumped on top of the boxes and looked up. Overhead there seemed to be some sort of a shelf.

As I worked my way up the stacked boxes, I realized they were resting on a narrow stairway. I climbed to the top. The runway went the width of the room, and at the far end there was a door. I charged toward it, found the handle and twisted. It was locked. My foot lashed out, smashing into the door near the latch. The door broke free and swung open.

My pocket flash pierced the darkness, finding another walkway but no stairs leading downward.

"Lily, quick, come here."

She looked up in surprise, then, excitedly ran up the stairs. Cautiously we crossed the first building, then the second. At the third one the door opened to the soft night sky. Below was an alley. I hung over the edge of the roof and dropped to the ground.

I caught Lily as she jumped and led her to the car. We drove away slowly. Behind us we could see the flames from the bookstore and hear the sirens in the distance. When we were safely away from the mob, I stopped the Mercedes and leaned back my head.

I took a deep breath and practiced the self-hypnosis tricks I'd learned back in the States. A few seconds in the shallow trance relaxed me. I felt as if I were coming out of a long, refreshing sleep when I heard Lily speaking softly beside me.

"We always knew this would happen," she was crying.

"Who?"

"My father and I. When he agreed to work for your people, he said someday he would die . . . violently. It was the price we had to pay to stay out of the streets, to have a home and food. Now we have paid."

I wanted to say something soothing, but I couldn't find the words.

"Where will you go? Do you have relatives?"

"Could you take me to my uncle?" she asked. "Perhaps he will care for me."

I nodded and she gave me an address. It was only a few blocks away. I let her off in front of an imposing building on Old Court House Street.

"He will be working late," she said. "He always does."

As she slipped out of the car, I gave her the name of my hotel. "If I can help you, Lily, call me."

She looked at me steadily through those strange green eyes and managed a small smile. "Mr. Matson, you have already helped me as much as the gods will allow. You saved my life."

She turned and ran for the doorway.

Back at my hotel I checked the suite in case I had

had an uninvited visitor. Everything looked okay. I turned on the radio as I showered and dressed.

While I knotted my tie, I heard Radio Calcutta reporting another political bombing. This time the home of the Russian vice-consul had been hit, and the Communists were in a rage.

"The Soviet consul, Alexander Sokoloff, today demanded that federal Indian troops strengthen defenses around every Soviet official's home and every Soviet-related business in Calcutta," the newscaster reported. "Sokoloff further demanded the ouster of all American consulate personnel from the city unless the attacks against Soviet personnel and property are stopped immediately."

I whistled softly. That was new in diplomat circles. I had never heard of one country asking another to oust the diplomats of a third power. The implications were awesome. No wonder Hawk and the State Department were concerned.

But why the attacks? I still had no idea why anyone would start heaving bombs at the Russians. And why in Calcutta?

Maybe that question was easier. India was the showplace of democracy in Asia. The British had left a structured system that worked very well in some places and was adequate in others. But it had failed miserably in Calcutta.

Perhaps Chuni Mehta could give me the lead I needed to discover who was behind the trouble.

Finding her address wasn't hard, although it wasn't

in the phone book. A couple of calls and I was on my way.

She lived in one of the oldest "palaces" on Chowringhi Road, a princely affair set back from the road in a huge plot of land with a high steel fence around it and blue ceramic tile on its roof. There was a driveway up to an ornate but strong iron gate. A Sikh looked sharply at me, spoke into a telephone, then waved and opened the big gate. I drove through and heard it clang behind me.

I parked farther up the drive between a Rolls-Royce Silver Cloud and a battered Land Rover.

A young Indian girl waited for me and led me through a court, past a garden with screen overhead, down a path beside a swimming pool and through a door at the far side of the huge mansion.

Chuni had an apartment in a small section of the big house. She met me at the door.

"You found me," she said and smiled. "I was really hoping you would."

She turned, giving me the full benefit of the brilliant sari she wore. One arm and shoulder showed the soft, delicate blue of her blouse, most of it covered by the shawl that billowed from her left shoulder and under her right arm. It was a silken sheen of a hundred colors with an intricate pattern for a border and random figures hand-stitched into the silk. It swept to the floor in a swirl.

"Lovely . . . both the girl and the sari."

She smiled, letting her brown eyes study me.

"And you, sir, are handsome and expensively dressed, but the gun shows under your left arm. Do all American firecracker manufacturers carry guns?"

I laughed to cover my surprise. Most trained eyes can't detect Wilhelmina because she is tailored into my jackets. But this coat was one Hawk had brought me, and it wasn't as well cut as the others.

"In a foreign country a man never knows what he might run up against."

Chuni let it pass. She swept her hand around the room. "How do you like my place?"

It was interesting. A cross between bad modern and pop-art with overtones of black humor. I told her so, and she frowned at me.

"Don't be cruel; you should be nice to me."

"Why?"

"That's the way to impress a girl."

"Why should I want to impress you?"

"It's well known that American men try to seduce every girl they meet."

She nodded at someone I didn't see and steered me toward folding glass doors that opened onto a pleasant balcony. It was planted with flowers, small shrubs and a tree. Although I had come in on the ground floor, we were now two stories up, overlooking the river.

Below I could see the yellow flames of small fires.

"A funeral," Chuni explained. "Down at the burning ghats near the Ganges tributary, the Hooghly river."

I wondered if Chuni was on assignment now, if she knew who I really was and if she knew about the attack on our safe house last night? She gave no sign I could detect.

"The family brings the body to the river to be cleansed," she said. "Then the son will crush the skull."

"Crush the skull?" I asked incredulously. "Of the corpse?"

"Of course, to release the soul before the body is burned."

"And the ashes?"

"Thrown into the river by the Doms, the caste who tend the burning ghats for us. After they've sifted the ashes to find gold rings and such. It is the way they live."

She turned then and took a glass of sherry from the servant who brought a tray to us. I tasted the wine and found it excellent.

Soon the servant girl returned to announce the meal. I was expecting some fantastic Indian dishes, lots of rice and curry, but as Chuni said, we ate like the villagers. The meal was almost meager, in spite of the gold-trimmed dinner plates and the lavish silver service.

"*Sag,*" she told me as I bit into a green leafy vegetable. And *chapaties,*" she added as I cut a flat pancake-shaped bread with a fork. There was lentil sauce poured over rice and a few scraps of goat meat, but hardly the gourmet dinner I had expected in a home like hers.

Chuni explained, "Eating the simple food the villagers eat helps me remember I have earned nothing. Without my father's wealth . . . ," She paused and looked up. "Do you understand?" she asked.

I nodded. The misery, the poverty, the death one walks through daily on any Calcutta street brought the point home with clarity. I hoped this thoughtful, beautiful Brahmin girl was on our side.

After dinner we went into the living room, and she turned on the stereo. The music was Eastern, although I don't think she expected me to appreciate the dissonant sounds of the drums, the cymbals and the wheezing of the hand organ.

"I'm curious about you," she said as she stood across from me with her hands folded demurely in front of her. "I'm curious about a man who goes to such efforts to meet a woman he has never seen, a man who also carries a gun."

"You're not exactly transparent yourself," I told her. "Most beautiful women would rebuff such a clumsy pickup."

She laughed and started past me to the built-in bar on the far side of the room.

"Have you ever shot anyone, Mr. Matson?" she asked abruptly.

I caught her hand and turned her to me, pulling her in close. "Only beautiful girls who talk too much."

She was ready when I bent to kiss her. Her arms

went around my neck, holding my face to hers. The kiss began softly, then grew in power until our lips parted and my tongue lashed into her mouth. She sighed gently, then relaxed her arms and moved away from me.

"I think it's time we had a talk," she said. "We just met, and I don't know you and. . . ."

My lips touched the tender places low on her neck and her objections faded away softly.

A few minutes later we were in her bedroom, the door was locked, and I had just kissed her again. We were lying on the bed. Chuni laughed softly as she sat up and took off the beautiful long shawl of the sari. "Let's go swimming," she suggested.

"Are you serious?"

"Yes, of course. Right now." She licked her lips with the tip of her tongue. "Now you're supposed to say you don't have any trunks."

"I won't need any."

I helped her unbutton the blue blouse and found she wore no bra. Her breasts swelled ripe and full to the hard, dark nipples. She kissed me again, letting her lips cling to mine. She unbuttoned my shirt, and a moment later we were both nude.

She took my hand and led me gently through the house, down the steps to the pool. Lights were on at the deep end. A pair of chaise longues rested near the steps at the shallow side.

She ran to the edge and dove, slicing the water cleanly. I hit the water a moment later. Finding her under the surface, I swam to her, kissed her lips, then held her tightly. At last we broke to the surface, gasping for breath.

There was no reason to talk. We moved to the steps and I let my lips work down her cheeks to her throat, on to her chest and up the slope of her breasts.

She caught her breath as my lips closed around the pointed mounds. She slid into the water again, pulling my face down over the flat place below her navel.

Back at the steps a moment later her kisses trailed down my chest, then caressed my wet belly, moving lower until I moaned in delight.

I stood her up, cupped water in my hands and poured it over her sleek breasts, watching it tumble and slide down between and around the upthrust peaks.

She pushed me backwards into the water, then turned, half floating, legs wide in invitation, urging me forward. I glided ahead gently, moving my hands over her high, tawny mounds, exciting the flat nipples until they came tall and rigid, demanding. I bent down, my mouth moving from breast to breast until I heard her moan softly and reach for me.

I slid over her in the water like some prehistoric amphibian, pressing close, then thrusting hard and sure as she cried out in pain and surprise.

We both dipped underwater, still clasped together. Soon we surfaced. Her legs had lifted to circle my back. We floated with soft, gentle motions in a kind of basic rhythm that sent shock waves through both of us.

I heard her cry through our kiss just as we sank beneath the surface of the pool again. This time we rolled over, yet never slowed down.

I felt her arms thrust to push us upward. As we broke the surface Chuni moaned long and low, a kind of primeval sigh of satisfaction and release.

We paddled slowly back to the steps, still wrapped in each other's arms. For a time we lay looking at the stars, murmuring gently to each other.

It was twenty minutes later when we left the water, so relaxed and refreshed that for the moment I had almost forgotten why I was in Calcutta.

We dried each other and walked back to her bedroom on the top floor of the mansion where we could look out at the billion lights of Calcutta.

She brushed hair from my eyes.

"You're involved in much more than firecrackers, aren't you? You arrived in town this morning. You went to see the U.S. consul and then calculatingly met me. Why?"

I said nothing.

"Most American businessmen in Calcutta aren't allowed to drive the U.S. consul's personal car. I've seen it a hundred times. You must be something special. And Patsy at the *Calcutta News* is a friend of mine. She phoned this afternoon and told me someone had been asking about me." Chuni laughed softly.

"I had to play an extra set of tennis waiting for you to come." She kissed my nose. "I'm glad I waited."

My first panic faded. She could have found out all of this from Indian Secret Service, or she might have figured it out on her own. She was a smart girl. What she had said could all have come from simple observation.

I kissed her teasing lips. "Why is it beautiful girls always asked the damndest questions?"

"I have another one. Would you like to stay here with me while you're in Calcutta?"

We were both still naked. I looked down at her enticing body, kissed one full breast and said, "I'd like to spend all the time I possibly can with you, Chuni."

"Beautiful," she said and pulled my mouth back to her quivering breast.

An armed soldier stood guard at the entrance to my hotel when I arrived at two A.M. He wore a holstered pistol and had a rifle slung over his shoulder. He touched his hat in salute as I went past him.

The next morning I got up at nine when someone pounded on my door. A messenger stood there with a note. I was to call the consulate; it was urgent. As I dressed I switched on my transistor radio and caught the last of the Radio Calcutta news.

". . . and the consul said considerable damage was sustained by the building. Two other U.S. structures were hit during the night . . . the U.S. Information

Service Library and the American Express office in central Calcutta."

Obviously the situation had worsened overnight. The Russians in Calcutta were no longer the only targets. Now Americans were being hit too.

"No comment was forthcoming from the U.S. consul," the newscaster continued, "and police have refused to speculate on whether the latest incidents are linked to the recent bombings against the property of the Soviet Union. In other news from around the world. . . ."

I snapped it off, dressed quickly and called the consulate. It was Slocum, as I'd expected, and he wanted to see me at once. I was in his office ten minutes later.

From the window I could see where a small bomb had ripped a corner from the sprawling building. Workmen were already patching the damage, and police milled around in the debris.

As for Slocum, his self-assurance was shattered. His hands quivered as he tried to light a cigarette. The desk that had been so clean the day before was covered with papers and he had to search for an ashtray.

"You heard?" he asked anxiously. His white shirt hung open at the throat and he was unshaven. I had a hunch he was more receptive to men like me than he had been the last time we met.

"About the three bombings?"

"Jump that total to seven, including two of our cars

blown to pieces. The Russian consul was on the phone just now protesting his innocence. We have asked the ambassador in New Delhi for permission to request Indian troops to guard the consulate and various other U.S. installations."

Slocum stood and motioned for me to follow him. We went out to the curb and got into the Mercedes he had loaned me.

"I have something to show you I think you'll find interesting," he said. "I don't claim to know your real function here, but I understand I am to give you the best support and cooperation I can in this delicate matter."

He stopped the car half a block from a large stone building. Overhead fluttered the red flag with hammer and sickle. Three dozen armed Indian troops stood at guard posts around two sides of the building. Each of the entrances was protected with an offset barricade of sandbags. It looked like a set for a war film.

"Sokoloff, the Russian consul here, says he's prepared to take direct action if any more of his buildings are bombed. That was yesterday. Now he's yelping that he didn't have anything to do with the attacks on us."

"So the escalation has started," I said.

"This whole thing is snowballing, I saw it happen in Algiers. It gets rolling and suddenly it's going so fast and getting so big that nobody can stop it. Too many different factions fighting each other. If something doesn't stop this, we could be sitting on a powder keg. And if it blows, it could bring down the entire Indian government. Calcutta could soon be a city of dynamite with a thousand hooligans running around waving torches, competing with each other to see who can be the first to light the fuse. And we'll be caught in the center."

I looked again at the sandbag barricade and knew he was right. I wished I were somewhere else.

"You're planning to put guards around the consulate, aren't you?" I asked.

Slocum nodded. "We've hired fifty men and are arming them with rifles. We'll use them until we can get Indian troops."

"Good. Where can I find the bomb fragments the police picked up after the blasts?"

"They're with Amartya Raj, of the Police Department. He's also on the Save Calcutta Commission and adviser to the commanding general who runs West Bengal now under the Martial Law edict. He's a good man." Slocum wrote down an address and gave it to me.

"What about those supplies I asked for?"

"I had them put in the trunk," he said.

He drove slowly past the Russian consulate and headed back to his own office. He stopped at the curb, and I slid behind the wheel as he stepped out into the street.

I called him back and asked him to wait while I

scribbled out a top priority wire for him to send back to Washington for me.

I started the engine again, but he laid his hand on my arm and scowled thoughtfully.

"There's a meeting coming up that might interest you . . . a special session of the Save Calcutta Commission. Both Sokoloff and I have been invited. Must be ten or fifteen business, cultural and military leaders on the commission. It's an attempt to settle some of the problems that have been tearing the city apart."

"Sounds like a Chamber of Commerce meeting," I protested. "Hardly my specialty."

"A Colonel Chung Woo has arranged it. An interesting chap. He's big in shipping, steel too, and more than fifty other operations. He was with Chiang Kaishek when the old generalissimo was fighting the Communists on mainland China. He came to India when Chiang got whipped. Now he's a millionaire, a neat, precise little man with a lot to lose if Calcutta explodes. He tells me he has established a bridge of peace that we and the Russians can walk across."

"So where do I fit in?"

He wrinkled his brow as he sought an answer. "You're supposed to be a businessman, a munitions expert. It's logical that I'd make use of your talents as long as you're in the city. That's the excuse I'll give the police when I tell them you want to check out the bomb fragments for us. Besides. . . ." He hesitated and I could tell he was searching for the right answer. "Well, I mean, there's an element of risk in any meeting with the Communists under the circumstances. After all . . . that bomb at the consulate. . . . Well, it could have killed someone . . . me, for instance And you're . . . how should I say it . . . experienced in this sort of thing."

I let the amusement show in my eyes. He was scared and suddenly I was a valuable friend.

"Sure," I told him, "I'll be there."

"The House of Peace," he said. "A Chinese restaurant on Park Street."

He breathed a sigh of relief and told me the time. He was whistling as he reached the gates, and I had an urge to call out to him and tell him the truth. Having me around wouldn't protect him.

No one was safe, not in Calcutta, not as long as fifteen-cent bombs were exploding in every corner of the city.

CHAPTER IV

I could sense the growing tension in the city as I drove to the address I wanted on Old Court House Street. The crowds were spilling over into the roads. Only the towering double-decker buses seemed powerful enough to plow through the rivers of humanity, so I pulled in tight behind one and let it run interference.

During the last couple of blocks children along the curbs recognized me as an American and trotted beside the car, jeering and making crude remarks in colloquial Hindi that I didn't understand. Adults peered at me curiously, contenting themselves with dour expressions that suggested their growing hate for the foreigners who were causing so much violence in their city.

When I reached police headquarters, I was surprised to see it was the building where I had left Lily Mir the night before. Although it made sense, somehow it never occurred to me that her father might have been related to someone on the city's police force. An agent like Randy Mir would have needed contacts in government to be of any use to AXE.

In front the building was strictly official in appearance with traditional pillars and wide, well-worn steps where beggars lay idly waiting for donors. In the back were living compounds for the officials.

As I went up the broad stone steps, two security guards approached me. They politely asked what I wanted. When I told them I wanted to see Mr. Raj, they led me to a side door.

There was one secretary; then I was in a big office with a steel desk and filing cabinets and one bare light bulb hanging in the middle of the room.

Amartya Raj was an impressive man, over six feet tall and built wide and strong—unusual for an Indian. He wore a Western business suit but had an inchwide copper bracelet around each wrist.

"Ah, Mr. Matson," he began. "Your consulate called . . . said you'd be coming by."

He thrust out his hand and waved me to a chair opposite his desk.

"I'm here to buy fireworks and powder," I began, "but Mr. Slocum asked me to look into these terrorist attacks since explosives are my line."

A thin smile spread across the big Indian police officer's face and I knew he didn't buy my cover story for a minute, but apparently he had no intention of challenging me.

"Quite natural you Americans would want to bring

in your own people on this thing. We'll cooperate in any way we can."

"Could I look at some of the bomb fragments?"

"Certainly," he said, turning to a cabinet where he took out a rusty quart-size tin can. "This is a whole bomb that didn't go off, the fuse fell out."

It was almost identical to the one Hawk had shown me, except that small holes had ben punched in opposite sides and a long string tied to each hole.

"Forget about fingerprints, Mr. Matson," he said. "We have some partials, but very few of the eight million people in Calcutta have prints on file."

"What's the string for?"

"We don't know. Perhaps to carry it. In India we love to balance things. Women carry jars, baskets, even rocks on their heads. Small boys and girls tie a string to little objects to carry, such as a book or jar. Then they can swing the object on the string, make it go around, stop it, make up games as they walk."

Raj picked up the bomb by the string and showed how it might have been swung. "But I really can't imagine anyone swinging this thing like a toy."

"Any leads at all?" I asked.

Raj walked to the window. "We are not as efficient as your police in the United States. And we have eight million suspects. In Calcutta it is said you can buy a killing for ten rupees and hire a mob for fifty."

"Did you find anything this morning after the attack at the consulate?"

He shook his head wearily, then led me out of his office and down the hall to the police laboratory. For an hour he proudly showed me through the procedure they had followed as they painstakingly checked out each attack.

But when the tour was over, I knew nothing I hadn't known before. The bombs were all crude, hand-made affairs. Nothing but tin cans stuffed with potassium nitrate.

Raj shrugged helplessly. "A few bits of string, an old can . . . our terrorists leave nothing else. Quite frustrating. They seem to come out of nowhere . . . unseen, unheard—until the explosion hits."

He promised to keep me informed but eased me out of his building with such expertise that I left shaking my head. I was getting nowhere fast.

Then I saw Lily. She was coming across the court-yard from one of the houses in back of the police headquarters.

I turned away, not wanting her to see me, but she called and came running toward me. Before she reached me I saw the dog with her, a magnificent German shepherd, an animal with the strength of a powerful man.

"For you, Mr. Matson," she said as she stopped with the animal at her heels. She looked up at me with green eyes that still showed the shock of her father's violent death. She seemed surprised that I didn't understand at once. "It's Prince," she said. "My father trained him . . . he wanted you to have him."

The animal sat quietly at her side, and I remembered what Hawk had told me. Randy Mir had trained an animal to sniff out explosives.

"We had him in a kennel," she said. "I got him this morning. He's magnificent. He can. . . ."

I touched her arm and stopped her in mid-sentence. "All right," I said, "I'll take him."

Again she seemed surprised, but her gaze followed mine as I glanced up toward the window of Amartya Raj's office.

"Oh, yes, Uncle Raj. He has been good to me. But I will be leaving today to go to Madras. I have a married sister there whom I will live with. I will be fine."

I groaned to myself. If I had ever had a cover on this assignment, it was surely blown now.

"Does your uncle know about yesterday?" I asked. "Does he know who I am?"

She whispered "no" and said she would tell him only that I was a friend, that I had come to express my regrets about her father's death. Then she attached a leash to the dog and passed it to me.

"Take him," she said. "My father wanted you to."

She darted back to the house and left me alone in the driveway leading to the street. I could still see Amartya Raj watching me, but I pretended not to notice.

I walked briskly out to the car and tried to get in before I was again recognized as an American by the scrawny boys congregated around it. I would have made it, except the dog balked. When I opened the rear door of the Mercedes, he leaped back, yanking the leash from my hand.

He whirled and barked, seemingly confused. Unafraid, several boys closed in, shouting at me and taunting the animal with sticks. He showed his fangs but ignored the stones that hit him.

I ordered him into the car, but he ignored me. He ducked his head and sniffed, then bounded toward the small crowd of street urchins that surrounded me.

Suddenly he lurched at one boy, hitting the frail little body at shoulder height. The boy screamed and raised his hands to ward off the bared fangs. Blood squirted from the wound before I could leap at the animal and hook my fingers under his collar.

As quickly as it started, the attack was over. The injured boy scrambled to his feet and streaked away down the street. The others scattered too, and I stood alone at the car with Prince. He wagged his tail and beamed up at me as if he expected approval. I cuffed him once across the head, then shoved him in the back seat of the Mercedes.

"Damned animal," I said as I slipped behind the wheel. Like everything else in this assignment, he was worthless.

Since I couldn't get rid of him immediately, I kept him with me until I got back to the hotel. There I hired an untouchable to watch him.

With a few minutes to spare, I called Chuni. I wanted to say something about last night, but there was no answer, so I settled for flowers delivered by a sickly looking porter who smelled of *ganja,* the narcotic that eases the suffering of so many of India's poor.

I spent the next half hour telephoning every chemical factory I could reach, spreading the word that I was interested in buying five tons of potassium nitrate for use in my fireworks. I found only two firms that said they had export licenses and could supply me. I wrote down their addresses for a possible check later. I couldn't afford to pass up any remote chances.

At 11:30 I got back into the big Mercedes and drove to the House of Peace. I hadn't seen many Chinese in Calcutta, but the restaurant seemed to be doing a brisk business. Slocum stood just inside the door waiting for me. I was five minutes early.

"Our friends from the Soviet have not arrived yet," he said, as we moved past the tables to a room at the side which was set up for twenty people. "Colonel Woo has been bouncing around like an expectant father. He says he has tremendous faith in this little peace mission of his."

We heard the Russians before they arrived. A hearty, belly-whumping laugh echoed through the thin walls, followed by a thunderous voice.

"That's Alexander Sokoloff, the Soviet head man here," Slocum said. "His main job is spying." Then the door opened.

Sokoloff was short and heavy. He wore a thick, double-breasted suit and mopped sweat off his bald head with a handkerchief. For a trace of a second I saw a gleam of recognition stab past his eyes; then he stared at me as if he had never seen me before. He had. At least twice before I had met Sokoloff, or Volgint or Colonel Zero, and each time we had played the espionage game to a draw. But each time I had completed my mission and he had squirmed out with enough credit to save his neck back in Moscow.

Slocum made the introduction smoothly like the diplomat he was. His smile for Sokoloff seemed genuine, although I knew he hated the man and what he stood for. More people came, including Mr. Raj from the Police Department, who seemed to hold the respect of those assembled.

More introductions were made, and Woo came back. He was the only Chinese in the group. A small man with glasses, he fingered his small Van Dyke beard nervously as he went to the head table and motioned for everyone to be seated. He spoke in Hindi, and considering that he had been in India for over twenty years, his Hindi was poor.

"Gentlemen, this very bad time. Bad for business when bomb go off. Bad for Soviet, bad for American, bad for everyone."

Colonel Woo continued in his pidgin-Hindi for five minutes, telling of the great strides their commission had made in lowering tensions and establishing better communications with the military and civil rulers. Then he emphasized that all of their work would be lost if this confrontation between the United States and the Soviet Union was permitted to continue.

He motioned to an Indian waiter, who brought a stack of papers to him.

He bowed proudly and smiled like a smug man who is about to succeed where others have failed.

"Now have work out very fine solution," he said. "Is on paper. Please to read small statement carefully."

Woo studied all of us as we ducked our heads to read the agreement he had passed among us.

Momentarily I hoped he had a solution. If the little Chinese could intercede between the major powers, I might escape a messy assignment.

Then, with no warning at all, Sokoloff was on his feet screaming. I missed some of it, and most of his words were Russian, but I got the message. He was furious.

The Russians had thrown no bombs, he cried. It was all the Americans, trying to stir up trouble. And now someone was trying to trap him into admitting something they hadn't done.

I glanced down at Woo's proposed agreement and saw immediately what Sokoloff had meant. It was a simple statement that each country agreed to halt future attacks on any other sovereign nation or its property in the city of Calcutta for at least six months.

The American consul's reaction was slower and a little more dignified, but I could see the red flush working its way up Slocum's neck from his collar.

"Preposterous," he said. "An affront to my nation." He took the papers and ripped them in half. "The United States objects to this brazen suggestion that it has ever taken part in, agreed to, or otherwise supported any attack upon any property owned or operated by the Soviet Union in the city of Calcutta."

The room erupted around us. The Russian delegates noisily protested, and Raj, who had appeared so calm in his office, jumped to his feet and shouted in favor of the plan.

"Anything to stop this insane threat to our city," he cried.

And the lone Englishman at the conference, a pudgy banker with puffy eyes, leaned far out onto the mahogany table and mumbled.

"If you've thrown no bombs, why not support the ruddy plan?"

Slocum lost his cool.

"Because, you idiot, the paper says we will *stop* the bombings. That's almost an admission of guilt." Slocum spat out the words. "The whole idea is ridiculous. Why doesn't this commission find out who is doing the bombings? That would be a real service."

A dozen voices raised then. Sokoloff left his chair and moved nearer Slocum. They talked for a moment; then Sokoloff started to shout. A moment later Slocum was shouting too. First the language was Russian, then English, then Hindi, and finally a mixture of all three in a grinding sweeping tirade that settled nothing.

Colonel Woo sat at his chair, well below the flood of angry words, surprise and wonder on his small, round face. At last he stood, bowed slightly and left the room. His eyes held shock and disbelief.

Sokoloff let the Chinese leave, then pounded on the table with his big fists until he had the room quieted.

"Gentlemen, the Soviet Union will not sign this ridiculous pledge. It is an insult to us! It has been and will continue to be our position that the United States of America owes us the sum of twenty million dollars for loss of property and lives. As soon as this sum is paid, we will be glad to sit down and discuss other unfortunate aspects of this situation. Is the United States ready to repay the damages caused by its bombs?"

I felt Slocum stiffen in his chair beside me; then he stood, his eyes glaring at Sokoloff.

"Yesterday a bomb exploded in the U.S. consulate. Lives could have been lost, and we demand an official apology from the Soviet Union."

Sokoloff choked on the glass of water he was drinking. Before he could recover, Slocum touched my shoulder and we walked out the door.

Slocum waited until we were in the street before he started yelling. Surprisingly, his anger was at Colonel Woo.

"The idiot! Woo is a meddling moron. How did he think something so inane as that would work? Why didn't he leave diplomacy to the diplomats? Things now are worse than before. At least then we only yelled at each other over the phone."

I stared at him and realized how the problem was

mounting. The diplomats were shouting now. Too often in history that had been the prelude to war.

I tried to calm him, but he wouldn't listen. He grumbled something at me and raced off. Left alone in the street, I stood turning a gold-tipped cigarette over and over in my fingers. I kept trying to think, trying to sort through the meager facts I had at my disposal. I didn't know exactly where to start, and I had a gnawing suspicion that time was running out faster than anyone thought.

In desperation I went back to the hotel.

I parked my car in the rear and started toward the lobby before I saw Prince romping and playing on the other side of the lot. The untouchable I had hired to watch the animal lay asleep in the warm sun, but four boys teased and petted the dog like a family pet. My first reaction was to warn the boys. Then I realized the powerful shepherd was wagging his tail and scampering around like a pup.

It was hard to believe the same animal had tried to tear an arm from another child only hours before.

A half-formed thought flashed through my mind, and I looked at the animal again. He was having too much fun with the children to notice me.

Feeling almost foolish, I slipped Wilhelmina from her resting place and extracted a single 9mm shell. I searched the ground around me until I found a crack in the concrete wide enough to hold the lead end of the bullet. I worked the brass casing back and forth until it pulled loose from the lead.

The gunpowder spilled out on the concrete, and I looked toward Prince.

The big dog stopped his playing, sniffed the air once and bared his teeth, then he flew at me, bounding across the lot in giant strides that left the children behind him staring in bewilderment. He came at me in one final leap.

I could have sworn his jaws were open a foot. His teeth glistened in the sun, and I made a dive for the nearest door.

I got inside just ahead of him. I could hear his heavy bulk smashing against the door behind me. His growling was deep and threatening. I was glad two inches of heavy wood separated us.

But I had learned something. Prince had attacked me just as he had the boy in the street outside Raj's office. I could only guess, but I was sure the boy and I had something in common . . . something that enraged the highly trained anmal—the smell of explosives.

It didn't make sense at first, but tied in with the few other facts I had it began to form a pattern.

I remembered a boy knocking against me just seconds before the explosion ripped through the building ahead of me as I came into town. And I remembered the strings that someone had used to carry the bomb that Raj had shown me at his office. Someone had carried it like a toy, he had surmised. A child, perhaps.

It was a slim lead, but I had to follow it through. So I slipped out to my car as soon as Prince was

tracted and drove back to police headquarters where
I had visited Raj's office. For an hour I sat in the
Mercedes, hoping to see the boy the dog had attacked
so viciously earlier in the day.

I hated to waste the time, but I knew no other way
to pick up the thread that I needed so desperately.
There were so many children along the street, hundreds of them it seemed.

I had almost given up when I saw the boy. He was
like most of the others—dirty and dressed in short
pants a dozen sizes too big for him—and I wouldn't
have recognized him if I hadn't seen the soiled band-
age wrapped around his wound.

I knew his kind. He was one of the *chowlee*—the
orphans who roam every city in the Far East, their
bony hands always outstretched for charity. The pathetic, hungry look in their eyes is their stock in trade,
but they'll take your gifts with one hand and pick your
pocket with the other. Survival is their only morality.

When I called to him, he backed away. Then he
ran, disappearing momentarily into the crowd. I let
him think he had lost me before I began to tail him.
For such a lean, sickly looking child, he moved fast,
leading me off the main street and into a neighborhood of mud-brick shanties crowding in around a
garbage-filled canal.

I lost him only when he disappeared into the tiny
shop of a copper merchant several blocks from the
police headquarters where I had first seen him.

He was gone only a moment. When he reappeared,

he was smiling and he clutched several rupee notes in his hand. He ran off, and I let him go, hoping I'd found a better lead now.

When he was gone, I crossed the street to the shop. The stone building was old, probably built while the British sipped tea in the afternoon and watched the untouchables die in the street outside their iron gates. Inside it was cool and dark. I closed the door and let my hand slip under my jacket to the place where my luger rested.

Something moved to my left, but I kept the gun in its holster. I was nervous, though there was nothing tangible to arouse my suspicions. The shop could be completely harmless.

"Sahib?" a man's voice said from the darkness ahead of me.

When my eyes grew accustomed to the dim light, I could see the shopkeeper. He was older than his voice sounded. His head was shaved and he wore a pure white robe. White paint made an inverted V on each cheek. A long, thin needle protruded from his shoulder.

"I'm looking for some heavy copper candlesticks," I told him in Hindi.

He shook his head. His eyes would not meet mine. His hands fussed with his robe, then began to shake.

"Go," he said in Hindi. "We have no candlesticks, and I beg you to leave me."

By now I could see better in the gloom. A beaded curtain showed at one side. I moved toward it. Wilhelmina slid into my hand. Quietly I checked behind the curtain. It shielded only one room used as living quarters. No one was there. I moved toward the other side of the room, where a solid door was set into the rock walls.

He rose in fear. Suddenly he spoke in perfect English.

"No, Sahib, I am but a simple merchant!"

As I pushed him aside, I heard the all too familiar crack of a bullet. Splinters flew from the paneling in the door and a slug whispered between the old man and me. Two inches either way and one of us would have been dead.

I fired through the door twice, then a third time. I heard a high-pitched scream of pain and stopped firing. As I kicked open the door, I was ready to shoot again, but my assailant was no longer a threat.

I stared down in disbelief.

Slumped on the floor of the small back room lay Lily Mir.

Her eyes blinked up at me. Her hands were on her leg, trying to stop the flow of blood from the bullet hole in her thigh.

CHAPTER V

Lily looked up at me, fighting the pain. My bullet had slashed through her thigh, going in one side and out the other. Luckily, it had missed the bone, but still she wouldn't be walking for a month. Her gun lay on the floor. I kicked it aside and watched her bite her lip to keep from crying. Her fists balled in fury.

"Mr. Matson," she cried. "I thought you were Zakir. I thought. . . ." She closed her eyes and whimpered. "I wanted to kill him . . . not you."

The pain overpowered her, and she doubled up over her wound.

An old Indian woman came out from the back room and studied the girl curiously. She disappeared for a moment and came back with a clear liquid that she sloshed over Lily's wound. I helped her, applying pressure to stop the bleeding. With a strip of cloth, the old woman wrapped the wound before she spoke.

"Are you her lover?" she asked.

When I shook my head, the crone appeared amused.

I heard the shop door close and realized the old man had left. To get help, no doubt.

I couldn't afford to wait. He might bring back the police, and I had no time to explain the shooting.

I picked up the girl in my arms and carried her outside, where I hailed a rickshaw and stuffed the man's hand with rupees. He raced us back to my Mercedes. From there I drove to the hotel, carried Lily in the back way and sneaked up to my room. I closed the door and locked it before I laid her out on the bed and checked the wound again.

She was going to need medical attention. Slocum was the only one I could turn to for help. He'd have to arrange it on the sly, since I couldn't afford to get involved. After I had called him and explained, I returned to the bed and slapped Lily's cheek lightly.

"Wake up, Lily," I said as I patted her cheeks. "Your little sleep is over."

"Mr. Matson, I'm sorry," she apologized as she came awake.

"Don't worry about it. I just wish I hadn't hurt you."

"I thought you were Zakir," she added. "I went there to find him."

She closed her eyes again, and I realized she didn't want to tell me the whole story. I had a guess at what troubled her.

"Your father worked for this Zakir, isn't that true?" I asked.

She nodded weakly.

"Your father sold us out, didn't he?"

"I think so," she said. "He told Zakir you were coming. He said your name wasn't really Matson. He said you would try to stop the bombings. That's all I know."

"And you blame Zakir for your father's death?"

"Yes. This is how he works. I know him."

"What about the boy?" I asked. "What does he have to do with Zakir?"

"Boy? I know nothing of a boy. But the copper merchant's shop belongs to Zakir. He goes there sometimes."

"What else do you know about Zakir?"

"Only his name . . . Zakir Shastri. He sells children. That's all."

I frowned, more confused than ever. "Sells children?"

Lily's eyes glazed and I thought she was going to faint again, but she sucked in her breath and spoke softly.

"Orphans, children of the street. He feeds them and then sells them to the rich as servants or to the brothels. He even sends some to the temples."

She drifted off again, half awake, half lost in her pain. Still I pressed her for details. I had to know where to find Zakir. She squinted up at me again.

She said something in Hindi I didn't understand, then I heard her murmur an address and say "a factory. My father met him there once." She closed her eyes. "I had to try to kill Shastri before I went to Madras. I'm sorry. . . ."

Her head tipped back and I knew she would answer no more questions for hours.

I checked the address she had given me with the ones I'd written down earlier, when I had been calling local chemical companies. My memory had served me well. The address she gave me was the same as that of the West Bengal Chemical Company, one of the big firms that did produce potassium nitrate. I was getting someplace at last.

I considered waiting for the ambulance, but decided against it. I would have to trust Slocum to get her to a hospital.

The chemical plant was located far up on the north side of the city in a slum where pigs rooted amid coconut husks and other garbage along the muddy street. There was no direct route to the spot I wanted to find. I settled for a clear view of the plant entrance across the street and half a block down. I climbed on top of a pile of rubble that had once been a building.

I wanted to appear inconspicuous, but my western dress made that impossible. Even the crows who flapped away from the rubble hovered overhead and seemed to watch me nervously. Several children eyed me until I crawled back through a hole in the old building to a point where I could watch the entrance without being seen too easily.

I didn't know precisely what I was looking for, but I wrote down a brief description of the three men who entered the plant while I watched. Almost by chance I spotted a small, brown-skinned boy cautiously approaching the rear yard of the plant from a side alley. A chain link fence with barbed wire at the top surrounded the entire property, but the boy hardly hesitated.

Looking from side to side, he lifted some brush from the bottom edge of the fence and slipped quickly through a small hole in the soft soil. He slithered quickly underneath several cars in the plant lot, crawled close to the building and began digging in a mound of trash.

Seconds later he came running back to the short tunnel under the fence. As he ran past me, I saw the glint of sunlight on tin. I considered stopping him, then decided against it.

I was sure the can he carried was filled with potassium nitrate. That would explain a lot of things . . . why the police hadn't traced the source of the explosives used by the terrorists, for instance. The explosive business is so closely regulated that the bombers might have difficulty buying what they needed, but a man working in the plant could easily steal small quantities of the explosive and leave it in the trash barrels outside the building. And who would think much of a child searching through trash? No one . . . not in the Far East where scavenging is an accepted profession.

The plan was a clever one. Even if I captured one of the kids, I would learn very little. They probably knew their contacts only as men who handed out food or a few rupee notes. My next step would be to take a look inside the plant, but this wasn't the time for that, not in daylight.

So I circled around to my car and drove back into town. I went straight to the consulate.

I slammed on the brakes when I saw the crowd outside the building. There were police cars and fire engines with men pouring water on the burning hulk of another Mercedes.

"Slocum," I thought as I parked the car and ran toward the excitement.

The still smoldering remains of the car hunched on the street with all four tires burning. The interior had been gutted, the hood blown off and the seats pulled out in a smoldering pile on the street. From the way the rear doors were blown off their hinges, it looked as though someone had planted a bomb in the back seat.

I pushed my way closer, expecting to see Slocum's shattered body lying in the street, but the body I saw there was not his.

It was a boy, his arms folded across his chest, his mouth gaping in surprise, his eyes still open. He was dead, lying in his own blood. Probably delivered the bomb and didn't get away in time, I figured.

"Matson," I heard someone say to me from the curb.

I looked across and saw Slocum standing just outside the gate to the consulate. His face was pale with fear.

"That could have been me," he said, nodding at the dead boy.

I went with him into his office where he sank into his chair and covered his face with his hands. His body was shaking.

"Pull yourself together," I told him. "This is going to get worse before it gets better."

"We need protection," he said. "Troops. Marines, maybe. I don't want to get killed. I have a wife and children."

I tried to calm him, but he wouldn't listen.

"You don't understand," he said. "It's almost the fifteenth, the fifteenth of August."

No, I didn't understand. "What's significant about the fifteenth?" I asked.

"Independence Day. August 15, 1947, the British officially pulled out."

"So?"

"Don't you remember? There was chaos then, rioting, Indians and Moslems streaming back and forth across the new border with Pakistan. Pure hell. Some say more than a million people died. It could happen again."

I looked across the desk at the calendar on his wall. It was the eleventh of August.

Now more things fell into place. The timing made sense. Whoever was behind the bomb attacks had planned carefully. They were slowly stirring the city in a cauldron of trouble. They were pitting two world powers—Russia and the United States—against each other. By the fifteenth the passions of the Indians would be at a fever pitch.

I looked at the calendar again. Less than four days left. Not much time.

I felt the perspiration beginning to form on my forehead and I could see the little lines of fear at the edges of Slocum's mouth.

He was right. There was plenty of reason for panic.

CHAPTER VI

Two hours later I was back in my hotel room. I tried to call Chuni, wanting to see her before I got too involved in the assignment, but again there was no answer. So I had to settle for work.

I changed clothes, putting on a black, long-sleeved shirt, a pair of black pants and solid hiking boots. I strapped the Luger under my shirt and put on the special belt.

I pocketed the spare clips for Wilhelmina and a hand grenade from Slocum's ammo box and went to the street. Tonight I didn't want the Mercedes to attract attention so I left it in front of the hotel and caught a rickshaw.

It was fully dark now. The street was not one of the main ones, but every spot on the sidewalk was occupied with sleeping bodies. I could pick out whole families huddled together in the warm, muggy air of Calcutta. I moved to the center of the street and walked quickly toward the chemical firm. It was only two blocks now.

Before I went around the corner, I scouted the next street. There were no lights here, just the murky glow of a pale moon.

No lights showed in the factory, either, I saw no guards. I slipped down one more block and came to the fence around the back of the building. I cut through it easily and stepped inside the unlighted yard. I expected some kind of security precautions at the plant, but I saw none.

The building itself didn't seem difficult to enter. There were no sky lights or big vents, but the rear door had nothing more than a standard lock.

Quietly I slid into the shadows and made my way to the door. It had an old spring-loaded bolt that offered no challenge. Ten seconds later I had slid the bolt back with the point of my knife and had the door unlocked. I opened it cautiously, listening for any alarms, any whining sounds or clicks, but there was nothing. I closed the door and eased the lock back in place. It was black inside the room. I crouched there for a moment before moving forward.

At the far side of the room I heard a door open, Then close. Slowly a form moved toward me. There seemed to be no threat; the man was crossing the area quietly.

I waited for him, and when he was in the proper position, my right hand came down sharply against the back of his neck. I wasn't trying to kill him, just to put him out of action for a few minutes, but I missed the exact spot. He slid sideways and directly into an old-fashioned left hook that smashed into his jaw. His head snapped back hard. It put a glaze over his brown eyes as he slumped to the floor.

Quickly I searched him and found no identification. The stout nylon cord I carried worked well, binding his ankles and hands. Then I carried him to the back door and began my tour of the plant.

I found no more guards. My pencil flash told me the story in a hurry. It was a small company. From the looks of it, the only thing they made was potassium nitrate. A short assembly line had been set up against one wall to produce the soft brown putty.

The only explosive left out in the open was half-finished stuff in one large kettle device that held ten gallons at most. Everything else was inside padlocked enclosures surrounded by wire fencing, but I saw immediately how the thefts had been handled. A long stick with a metal cup attached to the end lay outside one enclosure.

Someone patiently scooped small amounts from the open containers inside the enclosures, never taking enough to be noticed from any one barrel.

Only someone with plenty of time alone in the plant, like the night watchman, could accomplish the slow, tedious thefts.

I considered the possibilities for a moment before I made a decision. The plant had to go. If it was the terrorists' only source of supply, I could accomplish my mission with a minute's work. If it wasn't, I could at least reduce their capability.

So I found a roll of fuse and cut off a three-foot section. I sliced my way into the wire enclosure, fixed one end of the fuse in the nearest barrel and lit it.

I figured I had a full three minutes, but as I put my lighter to the end of the fuse, it sputtered and sparkled at twice the speed I expected. I leaped and ran toward the night watchman, wanting to carry him out into the open air before the explosion tore the building apart.

Unexpectedly, his feet came up and smashed me in the belly. I grunted and fell back. I could see the fuse sparkling in the darkness, half its length already gone.

Straightening up in spite of the pain in my gut, I stumbled back to the little man on the floor and tried to hoist him over my shoulder. He kicked and squirmed as though he were fighting for his life. There was no telling what he thought I was trying to do. I shouted at him in English and then in Hindi. I even pointed at the fuse and made a noise like an explosion, but nothing convinced him. He kept fighting as best he could with his legs and hands tied until I chopped him across the side of the neck with a blow that could have killed him.

Less than a foot of the fuse was left by the time I had him over my shoulder. He came to again and beat at my back with his fists. At the door he stuck out his arms and legs, blocking my attempts to escape.

He was snarling and cursing with determination. I could still hear the sizzling fuse behind us. I shouted at him, almost begging him to stop resisting.

Then with one desperate burst of energy I knocked his head hard against the door frame, stunning him long enough to get us outside.

A second later the barrel of potassium nitrate blew. A brilliant flash lighted the night sky; then came the thunder of a thousand bolts of lightning as the guts of the explosion ripped apart the small building and threw boards, cans and bits of metal into the Indian heavens.

The concussion socked us hard, knocking us a half dozen steps ahead. The Indian took the brunt of the concussion, and he fell on top of me, serving as a shield as the debris landed around us.

When I rolled from underneath him, he was still mumbling curses at me, so I dragged him through the fence and carried him into an alley before the people in the neighborhood began pouring from their ramshackle homes.

There was no fire, and I figured I had a few minutes before the police arrived to start searching the area. I rolled the night watchman over and learned close enough so he could hear me whisper over the shouting of the people in the street.

"The smallest sound, my friend, and you enter the endless circle of reincarnation. Understand?"

He nodded, and I carried him farther into the alley and then into a small courtyard which had an old truck parked in it. I put him down and propped him up against the truck's wheel.

"Now, you will talk, or you will be floating down the Hooghly River before morning."

He glared at me.

"Who hired you to steal from your employer?"

Silence.

"Who hired you to put the stuff in the trash?"

Silence.

I reached into my pocket and took out a small case I don't often use. It holds a hypodermic needle and three vials of chemicals. I let the guard see what I was doing.

Carefully I broke the hypodermic covering and took it out, then put the needle through the rubber stopper of the first vial and drew out the fluid.

"Have you seen something like this before?" I asked the man against the wheel. His face was rigid, his eyes wide in fear.

"This is a new drug called novocaine. Actually it's a truth serum that works beautifully. But it always kills the victim. I have no choice; I must know who hired you to help make those bombs."

He was shivering now. I tested the needle with my finger, then put it against his arm. He tensed and fell sideways.

"One last time, friend. Who hired you to give explosives to the children?"

"I . . . I don't know." He was sweating now, his

eyes watching each movement I made with the needle.

"You won't feel anything at first. Then the numbness starts. It gets worse, and soon you can't feel any pain at all. The end comes soon after that."

I tested the needle again. "Don't worry about it. I know what loyalty means. In half an hour you'll be dead, and your boss will be scot free . . . for a while. But by then I'll know about him too."

He shook his head. I plunged the needle into the muscle of his arm and shot the fluid in quickly. The needle was out and thrown away before the Indian realized it. He looked down at his arm, feeling the coldness of the fluid. A moment later the drug began to take effect and he turned.

"Zakir Shastri . . . he paid us."

"Any other names? Who does Zakir work for?"

The man shook his head.

"Were you the only source, or are there others who supply Zakir?"

"I know only one. South Calcutta Potassium on Kashmir Street."

"You sure that's all you know?"

He nodded.

"Feel your arm." I cut the cords around his wrists so he could touch the spot where I had injected him. "Can you feel anything there? That part of you is already dead."

His eyes flared in panic.

"Any other names you know? Any other chemical firms making bombs?"

He shook his head, still staring at the numb spot on his arm. I took Hugo and sliced the cords around his legs.

"There's only one way to beat the juice I shot you with. You have to run three miles. If you get out in the street and run hard for three miles, it will burn up the poison in your system and kill the novocaine."

He stood up, flexed his legs and touched his arm again in surprise.

"Go on, see if you can run it out; you've got a chance to still be alive by morning."

The small Indian stumbled the first few steps out of the alley, then ran like a whirlwind.

He shouted to the crowd outside the wrecked building, and I didn't wait to see if he referred to me. I ducked down another street, then made my way back to the hotel.

I was planning on a hot bath and a good meal before I checked out the other chemical plant the watchman had named. But when I got to my room, it wasn't empty.

As soon as I stepped inside, Chuni Mehta swung a small caliber pistol at my chest.

"Sit down and be quiet," she said.

CHAPTER VII

Chuni held the pistol in both hands, the way some professionals are trained for accuracy.

"What's the joke?" I asked, but there was no humor in the cold way she stared at me.

"The joke is me," she said. "I believed you."

A smile formed on my lips. I had used it before on an angry woman. Usually it worked.

"You're not Howard Matson. You're an agent for the United States government."

I shrugged. "So? You guessed that when we met."

"You're Nicholas Huntington Carter III, Nick Carter, Killmaster for AXE. You aren't even wearing a disguise. You made a fool of me."

"How?"

"I had to be told," she snapped, "by Raj."

"Your boss?" I guessed.

She didn't answer but the idea fit. I knew she was a new agent with India's slowly emerging intelligence setup. And I could tell she was a beginner.

"We're on the same side, why point a gun at me?"

"The bombings," she said. "Raj thinks you might be involved, maybe you're directing the whole thing. We've got a lot of questions to ask you."

When she paused, I recognized a quiver in her voice. She wasn't a pro yet, a seasoned agent who can kill without remorse.

"You think you can kill me and stop the bombings?" I made it sound like a joke, a fantastic child's idea.

"I can kill you if I have to," she insisted. "If you don't give me the answers I want."

I shook my head. "You've never shot a man before, have you? You've never pulled the trigger and watched him die. You think you can start with me?"

I kept my attention on her face, trying to measure her expression. My life depended on it. Would she really kill me? I doubted it, but I couldn't afford to be wrong. I wasn't ready to gamble my life here.

Guns have been pointed at me many times, and I've always been able to judge that instant when my adversary's attention is diverted ever so briefly. An unexpected sound, a flash of light; any distraction is worth the gamble if you're sure the man behind the gun is ready to kill you anyway. But with Chuni I preferred to wait.

"I came to Calcutta to help," I said. "I have orders to stop the terrorists before the trouble spreads any further."

"Then why do you come under an alias?" she asked. "Why not come openly, honestly?"

I had no real answer. "It's our way," I told her. "Secrecy."

"There is no trusting you," she said. "I should kill you while I can."

Her tone disturbed me. She seemed almost convinced. Maybe I had misjudged her.

I caught myself sucking in breath, waiting for the hot poker of lead to puncture my lungs.

I still hadn't breathed nearly a minute later when the phone rang on the table near my hand.

It rang three times before she motioned to me with the pistol. "Answer it," she said.

Turning halfway from her, I scooped up the phone with my left hand. The movement gave me a chance to get Hugo down into the palm of my right hand. I was no longer helpless.

"Yes," I said into the phone.

The voice that came through the receiver seemed surprised, as though the caller didn't expect me to answer my own phone.

"Ah, Mr. Carter, it is you."

The use of my real name hardly shocked me, but the caller's name did.

"This is Colonel Woo," the Oriental businessman's voice continued.

"You called me Carter," I said.

I glanced across the room at Chuni and formed the colonel's name on my lips for her benefit. She understood and whispered an explanation as I covered my mouthpiece for a moment.

". . . a friend of Raj's," she said.

I cursed to myself. Obviously, Raj was free with the information about my identity. I wondered why.

"Are you alone, Mr. Carter?" Woo asked.

I considered Chuni and the gun she held in her hand. "No," I told the Colonel. "Miss Mehta is with me. Perhaps you know her."

Chuni lowered the gun and slipped it in her purse, the reaction I'd expected. She wouldn't shoot me now, not when someone else knew we were together.

"Ah, yes. Very fine lady. Her father is guest in my home many times."

"You didn't answer my question, Colonel Woo," I said, pressing the point. "Why did you call me Carter?"

His sing-song voice hinted at amusement. "Most honored to know famed agent," he said. "Most sorrowful too about meeting this noon. Colonel Woo has failed. Has caused more anger between diplomats of great powers. I tell myself I must apologize to meeting guests. Then honorable police tells Woo his guests include famous American agent with same mission . . . to save Calcutta from terrorists. I have much sorrow, Mr. Carter, for our city. Must help stop bombings. Most important to adopted homeland. Most important to business."

"Thank you, Colonel. I'm sure the powers involved appreciate your concern, but this is a job for professionals. Time is running out."

"True, Mr. Carter. But perhaps humble businessman can assist great powers. I have much knowledge of India. I help police often. Would welcome opportunity to assist most famous American."

I hesitated only a moment. Perhaps the old Chinese was right—maybe he could help me.

"Would welcome you as guest in my home tomorrow," he said. "You and Miss Mehta. We talk. Maybe help save our city."

I agreed, and he set a time for dinner. Then I replaced the phone and turned to Chuni. She was still in the big chair across the room. The Western-style skirt hunched up over her thighs, showing the perfect shape of her legs. Hugo felt cold in my hand. I remembered how recently I had considered killing her. What a waste it would have been. But it wasn't necessary. She was no killer. The Indian government wasn't deeply enough into international espionage yet to need hired assassins. And even if it were, it would hardly send a rich, cultured girl to do the killing.

But she did have questions she wanted answered and she had thought a gun would be persuasive. Having failed with one weapon, she might try another, one I'd enjoy far more.

I returned Hugo to his home, put out my hand and lifted her from the chair. She kept her eyes away from mine as I pulled her against my chest.

"You bastard," she whispered.

My lips brushed her ear, then her cheek.

She was tall, and her body fit mine so well, her soft curves and indentations complementing the strength and hardness of my own. In another time and another place I would have told her that I loved her. But it wouldn't have been fair. For us there could be nothing more than physical passion. The only promises we could make would be for one night at a time.

As my fingers cupped around her swelling hips, her long, slender fingers were sliding down my back. Together we moved our bodies in a silent, mutual offering; then slipped apart and walked hand-in-hand to the bed.

"Lie down," she said. "Wait for me."

She stood in front of me to undress. When her soft, brown breasts swung free, I instinctively reached for them but she pushed me away until she was naked.

She knelt on the floor then and helped me with my clothes.

Still she wouldn't join me. She stayed on her knees, kissing me on the lips, then moving lower, ever lower, until my body begged to press against hers.

Her hands traveled over my body, feeling, touching, fondling. At last she moved up on the bed with me. She pushed forward slowly, resting her firm breasts on my chest, then swinging around her long lithe legs until she covered my body from head to toe.

She kissed me gently, then again with more fire. "Please, let me make love to you, my way."

The movement of her hips against mine convinced me. It seemed good having her on top, her hands

working at me, bringing me to a white heat before
I even moved.

Later we lay in each other's arms, looking through
the open windows at the lights of the city far below.

"Now," she said, "tell me the truth."

"You first. You work for Raj? True?"

"Yes, I work with him because I think I can help
my country."

"How?"

"To save the state of Bengal for India."

"The area around Calcutta?"

She nodded. "Yes. There are those who would
separate Bengal from the rest of the nation. Thev'd
form a new country or join with Bengladesh. Even
before the Bengalis broke away from Pakistan, there
were rebels in Calcutta who would tear our country
apart. The chaos caused by bombings might give
them the chance they need."

"And where does Raj think I fit into all this?"

"He doesn't know, but he doesn't trust Americans."

"What about you?"

"I don't know either."

I kissed her soft lips.

"We're both on the same side, whether Raj realizes
it or not. Just trust me for a while. A day or two,
maybe less."

She frowned skeptically. "Maybe," she said. "Maybe
I can for now."

"Good. Now, is there anything you can tell me that
will help? Does Raj have any leads on the supply of

potassium nitrate? Any hints about the organization behind it? Any man I can go after to hit at the very heart of the conspiracy?"

Chuni's pretty face wrinkled into a frown.

"I don't know. I just do what he tells me. You could ask him."

"No."

I tried to explain to her then. I didn't trust anyone, not even Raj. Actually I didn't trust her either, but I couldn't tell her that. As long as I didn't openly admit that I was an American agent operating inside his country, Raj was hampered by protocol. He couldn't arrest me or order me out of the country without proof. And his only proof so far was snuggled up naked in my arms.

"What will I tell him?" she asked.

"Did he ask you to kill me?"

"No, just to question you. The gun was my idea."

"Tell him what I know," I said.

I laid it out quickly, being careful to give her only the information I wanted to release. I mentioned the factory and the potassium nitrate thefts, but I said nothing about being involved in the explosion at the plant. Let Raj guess that for himself.

"There's a man named Zakir Shastri involved somehow," I told her. "Have Raj put his staff to work finding him. Police have ways of digging out people once they have a name."

I started to mention my suspicions about the kids delivering the bombs but changed my mind. I had told her enough already to gain her confidence. That's all I needed.

"You believe me now?" I asked.

"Yes," but there was still doubt in her eyes and I tried to assure her with a kiss.

She held back a moment, then let her hand slip down my body. Still naked we pressed together again and let our passions rule our bodies. Later she rose on one elbow and said, "Darling, I trust you, but please don't make a fool of me again. Don't lie to me any more."

"Never," I told her, wondering if she believed me. I felt no guilt—lying is part of my job.

"When it's over, darling, maybe we could go away. I have money, lots of it. I know Europe. You'd never have to work again in your life."

What she said surprised me. She sounded sincere. Maybe it was more than just an interlude for her. I rolled on top of her ready to make love again. She moaned in pleasure, and for a time we forgot there was a world beyond the room's walls.

CHAPTER VIII

The next morning we had breakfast in bed. The small Indian girl who served us seemed totally unaware that I was with a naked woman. When she was gone, Chuni rolled over, leaned across me and kissed my chest. I had to push her from under the covers.

While Chuni dressed, I called Slocum's office and asked for a number where I could reach Lily Mir. Lily seemed to be in good spirits when I spoke to her. She told me that she was being released from the hospital soon and would be going to Madras as she'd planned. I suggested that she take Prince with her when she left Calcutta. She agreed enthusiastically and said she would arrange right away for one of her relatives to pick up the dog.

I was glad I'd called her. So far my assignment had resulted in nothing but unhappiness for Lily. Maybe having the dog back would help her through the difficult adjustments that lay ahead for her. I wished her luck and hung up.

Then I turned my attention to Chuni.

We were going to stop at her place before driving out to Colonel Woo's. As I climbed into the front seat I realized that my mind was still too much on Chuni—I'd even forgotten to check the back seat. When I turned, a stiff male finger pointed squarely between my eyes.

"Pow, pow, Nick Carter, you're dead."

Chuni whirled digging her small pistol from her handbag. I had to stop her before she started shooting.

The man in the back seat reached quickly for his own weapon.

"Hold it, Sokoloff," I yelled.

The big Russian stopped, his stand still under his jacket.

"Who is it?" Chuni demanded. "What does he want?"

Sokoloff introduced himself. "Comrade Alexander Sokoloff," he said. "Consul to Calcutta for the Union of Soviet Socialist Republics."

"Bull," I said. "Tell her the truth, Sokoloff. You're a KGB spy, like most of the Russian diplomats around the world."

The Russian raised his hands in a gesture of surrender. "You Americans . . . always so pragmatic. All right, I am a spy. You should know. Correct, Mr. Carter? And you, Miss Mehta? You too are a member of our humble profession. Correct?"

Chuni frowned at me and refused to answer.

"It's of no importance," he said. "Today we are not enemies." He raised his hands again and tipped his head thoughtfully. "Tomorrow . . . who knows? Tomorrow we may kill each other, but today . . . today we must cooperate."

"Who says?" I asked coolly.

"I say so, Comrade Carter. We are in trouble."

"We?"

"All of us. You. Me. Miss Mehta. I have orders to kill you."

Chuni flinched, and I could see her hand tightening on the small pistol still in her grip.

I wasn't afraid. Not yet. I knew how Sokoloff worked. When he was ready to kill me, there would be no warning.

"I have orders to kill all agents who might be responsible for the terrorist attacks on our legation in Calcutta," he said. "Tomorrow you may have similar orders . . . to kill me and all the Chinese agents in the city, then the Indians like Miss Mehta . . . anyone who could be responsible."

"Why do you hesitate?" I asked. "You never had any qualms about killing before."

"Because I suspect it would do no good. I suspect the bombings would continue. I suspect neither of us is responsible. I suspect someone . . . how is you say . . . someone is working both ends against the middle."

I studied the Russian for a moment, and I almost believed him. He might be telling the truth . . . just this once.

"The tail is wagging the dog," I said agreeably. "And we're both looking like fools."

"Yah, yah," he nodded. "Is true. Someone causes trouble between us."

"How do we get out of it?" I asked.

The older man shook his head sadly. "I don't know But I have a new worry. We hear strange rumblings. We hear threats. There are those who say our consulate will be blown to rubble on the fifteenth . . . the day of independence."

"The streets will be full of people," Chuni added. "It would be a day made for violence."

"My government is angry," he said. "There is talk of retaliation—direct retaliation—if the consulate is damaged."

Perspiration formed around my collar. I hated to think what might happen if the threat was carried out.

"Why are you telling me this?" I asked. "Since when do you help the Americans?"

The Russian sighed. "Because I am told to stop you. Yet all I can uncover indicates you are not responsible . . . neither you nor any other Americans. Those who deliver the bombs are neither CIA nor AXE. They are. . . ."

He stopped and I finished the sentence for him. "They are children," I said.

Sokoloff nodded in agreement. "Yes, apparently they are children."

"I don't believe you," Chuni objected. "It couldn't be."

She protested, yet I could sense she was thinking back through the few facts the police must have told her.

"There was a boy killed outside the U.S. consulate," I said, "only yesterday."

"An innocent child," Chuni argued. "A passerby."

"A terrorist," Sokoloff suggested. "Using children ... it doesn't sound like you," he told me with a smile.

"Nor you," I said. "Not even the Maoists have stooped that low."

He slipped across the seat and opened the door. "That is all I have to tell you," he said.

When he was gone, I put the keys in the ignition, turned on the engine and drove to Chuni's place. While she changed, I stood on the balcony and watched the strange city stirring to life for another morning in its endless fight for survival. I wondered what kind of monster would bring more terror to the troubled city. Who had selected Calcutta for a battleground between the two great powers? What did he hope to gain?

I had no idea. Time was running through my fingers, and I was getting nowhere. Only three more days, and my leads were discouragingly thin. Whoever was using the children as terrorists had planned wisely. The trail was almost impossible to follow.

All I had was a name—Zakir Shastri. I could only

hope that Colonel Woo's widespread influence in the city could help me find the man behind the name.

When Chuni was dressed, we drove south toward the Bay of Bengal, following Colonel Woo's directions through flat delta country, where for thousands of years the mighty Ganges and its various outflows had been building up a rich protrusion into the bay. Woo's estate fronted on the Hooghly River. A massive, sprawling complex, it looked as though it too had been a long time in building. The estate covered the only rolling ground for miles and included thickets and hardwood groves and wide pastures for horses. The main house, made of pure white stone, glistened the sun like a temple.

When we stopped in a paved parking area at the massive front level of the house, two uniformed houseboys rushed up to open the doors of the car and ushered us through the big double doors into the main hall. For a moment I thought we had stepped into the past and were in the palace of one of the five hundred princes who had ruled the small states that now make up India and Pakistan.

The hall was unbelievably luxurious—the floor of finest marble and ceramic tile, pillars of pure marble, walls hung with brilliant ancient tapestries, furniture from all the antique periods of India.

The building was more a museum than a house, more a temple to all of India than a dwelling. Our guides lingered as we stared at the beauty, then moved us along gently through a door from the great hall to another room. This one was poorly lighted and was constructed of rough paving stone that could have been torn from the streets of a Chinese village. In the center of the room was a hovel, the roof four feet from the floor. It was made of cardboard, old boards, packing boxes, opened and cut apart tin cans and on one side the upturned bottom of a rowboat.

In the doorway of the shack sat Colonel Woo, wearing a dirty dhoti about his waist. He squatted in a basic yogi position.

When he saw us, he stirred but did not rise.

"Ah, have arrived. Pardon foolish memories. Was born in peasant hut like this," he said as he untangled his body. "Does soul good think back and say forevermore it shall be different."

He stood to his full height and bowed humbly. "Most honored you should grace my home, Miss Mehta," he said. "And you, Mr. Carter. Your presence exalts my humble position."

Chuni responded quickly, but I fumbled for words. Woo confused me.

The precise little man seemed embarrassed at being found in his peasant clothes. He excused himself and said he would join us in a moment when he was "more appropriately dressed for such distinguished guests."

He spoke quickly in Chinese and two young girls in Oriental dress appeared from another room. They bowed and minced ahead of us, their tight ankle-length skirts holding their steps to a matter of inches. They led us through another door and into a pleasant, Western-style room with soft music playing from a stereo, a TV set, carpeted floors, modern furniture, and a painting on the wall I swore was an original Pollock.

"Master say make comfortable; he will be here direct," one of the guides said. Then they both vanished through a door.

Over a massive fireplace hung a painting of Chiang Kai-shek in his younger days, when he still ruled mainland China. On an opposite wall was a second painting of equal size. This one was of Sun Yat-sen.

"Woo was not really a colonel," Chuni volunteered as I looked around the lavishly decorated room. "The title is an honorary one, given for his personal war against Mao and the Communists. He was hardly more than a boy when he served with Chiang."

I started to ask her more, but an Indian boy appeared in a white jacket and led us to the teakwood bar under the tiger-skin wall decoration. Like everything in the estate, the liquor supply impressed me. There were well-aged Scotches, fine cognacs, a superb collection of venerable rums. The boy offered them with no more hesitation than a bartender offers a beer.

We chose a Jamaican rum and were sipping at it when the colonel appeared wearing riding breeches and boots.

Micronite filter.
Mild, smooth taste.
For all the right reasons.
Kent.

America's quality cigarette.
King Size or Deluxe 100's.

Kings: 17 mg. "tar,"
1.1 mg. nicotine;
100's: 19 mg. "tar,"
1.3 mg. nicotine
av. per cigarette,
FTC Report Aug. '72.

He came to stand beside me, peering up at me, eager to please.

"Would enjoy ride before lunch?" he suggested.

I started to say that I didn't have the time, but Chuni agreed too quickly. He sent her off with one of the women servants to change clothes, while he led me into a short, statue-lined hallway. From the hall we circled an indoor swimming pool of clear blue water and went through a door and across a stone bridge that separated the interior section of the huge pool from the outside part.

Three horses stood prancing at the end of the small bridge inside a fenced bridal path, but he ignored them, waving his toward the private park on the terrace below us.

"Trap, perhaps?" he asked. "Or skeet. Your choice, Mr. Carter. To fill the moments until the lovely lady rejoins us."

A hint of suspicion stirred inside of me, and I looked at the small man's arms. They were unexpectedly strong and sinewy. In spite of his manicured nails, his hands were tough, like a peasant's.

"Trap," I said. "One of my better games."

He smiled. "Continental," he apologized, and suddenly I realized the style of his speech was changing. As he relaxed with me, he deliberately dropped the pidgin English he used to disarm his guests. "For more challenge . . . like life. One never knows what course the target of opportunity will take."

I didn't understand, but I followed him down to the

spokelike walks of the trap range and watched as two young servant boys trotted out to us, their arms loaded with selected guns.

"For a thousand rupees a bird," he said as he took an over-and-under Browning and stepped to the twenty-seven-yard marker. "Agreed?"

Before I could answer, he called for a bird, and the bright yellow disk streaked skyward. The Browning barked and the bird exploded twenty feet out from the small metal trap house. It was a good shot, clean and dead center, the kind that turns the clay pigeon into a starburst of fragments.

The little man smiled proudly and waited. I stepped to the line, inserted a shell in the single chamber of the gun I had chosen and called out to the boy at the control button. The clay bird streaked hard to the right. I raised the gun and fired. It powdered in mid-air, and I felt the fierce satisfaction of a clean kill.

Colonel Woo left me no time for gloating. He immediately called for another bird and fired, smashing it. I followed with an easy straight away.

We were shooting fast, rapidly enough that I worried about the boy in the trap house who had to lay the bird on the powerful throwing arm and get his hand out of the way before the heavy springs flung the target out into space. There was no rule that said we had to call for a bird and shoot the second the other man had shattered his own target, but without a word we'd set our own conditions.

By the time Chuni rejoined us, we were firing in a wild, exhausting rhythm, and our bodies were bathed with sweat. My arms arched from repeatedly lifting the eight pounds of steel and mahogany, and my shoulder smarted from the thumping of the recoil even though I bent my knees and leaned well into the butt. I was amazed at Woo. For a small man he seemed to suffer no more than I did. I could see the lust for victory showing at the edges of his mouth as I faltered and began chipping rather than powdering the birds.

"Dead and change," the boy behind us announced. "Seventy-five straight each."

"For ten thousand rupees," Colonel Woo cried out as he raised his gun for another shot.

He creamed the bird. My hands nearly shook as I raised my own gun for the seventy-sixth shot in rapid succession. I hit it and ten more before I felt the breeze hitting me at the back of the neck.

Woo felt it too late. The bird he had called for dipped unexpectedy just as he pulled the trigger. The yellow disk sailed triumphantly intact out into the littered plain in front of the trap house. It alone had escaped his weapon.

Colonel Woo held the gun at his shoulder for a moment, forcing himself to accept defeat. For an instant I saw demonic anger in those slanted eyes. Woo didn't lose gracefully, but when he faced me, he was again smiling, bowing, playing the role of humble peasant.

"Ten thousand rupees for the famous American." He

waved his hand, and a boy ran forward with a check-book. Woo scrawled out the amount and handed the check to me.

I accepted it, then held it in my fingers, intending to rip it into shreds.

"The pleasure was mine," I said.

"Wait," Chuni called from the edge of the trap field where she had been watching. She came running toward us and took the check from me. "For your children. Correct?" she called out to Woo for approval. "Ten thousand rupees should feed them for many days."

"Of course," Woo agreed. "For the children."

"*Your* children?" I questioned.

The small man laughed and pointed down the sloping hill toward a walled complex of buildings a quarter of a mile from us.

"The orphanage," Chuni explained. "He has saved hundreds of children from the streets. He feeds them, clothes them and gives them a home until they are old enough to take care of themselves."

"But there are so many more who need care," Woo said sadly. "Even a man with my wealth cannot help them all."

Woo pointed, and now I noticed the children on a field below us, hundreds of them, mostly boys, play-ing in the wire-enclosed yard of the orphanage. They made me think of the boy I had seen leaving the chemical company and the small broken boy in the street beside the bomb shattered Mercedes outside the American consulate.

I cursed my own suspicious mind. Woo was probably a generous philanthropist, but still I couldn't help suspecting him. I didn't want to believe he was involved in the bombings, yet that thought wouldn't go away.

"Perhaps you know the man I'm looking for," I said abruptly. "With your interest in children perhaps you know a man named Zakir Shastri. I understand he too takes children from the streets."

Colonel Woo hissed through his teeth. "That son of a serpent," he said in Mandarin. "I know him. He kidnaps children, uses them for his own purposes. I have rescued a few from his clutches, but there are always more."

Chuni frowned at me, probably wondering why I had mentioned Shastri. It had been a calculated risk to see Woo's response, but it was wasted. He had reacted as most people would, and I was still searching for a lead.

"Why do you wish to see him?" Woo asked. "Is he involved in the bombings?"

I shook my head. "I'm not sure . . . possibly."

"Perhaps we can be of assistance," Woo volunteered. "The children from the streets might know where to find this man."

He clicked his fingers and a servant boy trotted up beside him. Woo spoke to him at length in a dialect I didn't understand. He smiled triumphantly as the boy darted off toward the house.

"Will have children questioned," he said. "Some will know of this Zakir. Some have suffered at his hands. They will take you to him."

I nodded my thanks.

"But must play now," Woo announced as he led us to the horses.

We mounted the high-strung animals and pranced out along the bridle path to the point where the estate touched the banks of the river. He showed us his private marina and four sleek power boats, then led us around the handball courts of heavy plexiglass and up the path through the nine-hole golf course with its divot-free fairways and its unmarked greens.

"You have everything," Chuni remarked as we rode, and the small Chinese glanced across at me for agreement.

I thought I understood him then. He was a small man, feeding an enormous ego. The tennis courts, the golf course, the magnificent gardens . . . they were all virtualy untouched, unused, mere trophies to prove his own financial success. And we were there as his audience, invited to slap him on the back and tell him how great he was.

Although I needed his help, I gave in to an urge.

"Almost everything," I said perversely as I moved close to Chuni and leaned over to kiss her affectionately on the cheek.

Woo's reaction bewildered me. He laughed—a loud, throaty roar for such a small man.

"That too," he said, riding ahead of us toward the estate.

Inside the house he directed Chuni and me to different apartments on the upper floors. Fresh clothes were laid out for me there, and I showered and changed before going back downstairs.

Woo was waiting for me in his study, a two-story room paneled in exquisite woods and walled with a collection of first editions. He sat behind a huge desk that made him appear even smaller and more insignificant than he was.

Around him, sitting on the desk and on the floor before it, were girls. Ten of them, some Indian, some Oriental, some so fair-skinned I suspected they were full-blooded white.

"As I said," Woo smiled, "I have everything."

He waved his hand graciously over the heads of the solemn-faced girls.

"Take one," he said. "Take two. Be my guest."

CHAPTER IX

"I discovered quite early in life, Mr. Carter," Colonel Woo said proudly, "there are guideposts in man's trek to success. You can tell where a man is along the road by what he wants most. First, a full belly. Then things . . . materialism, you so aptly call it in your country. Next, with the first signs of great wealth, position. Later still, a cornucopia of sexual satisfaction. To the successful Arab, it's a harem. To the Japanese, the geisha. To the rich American, the mistress."

"And to the Chinese?"

He waved his hand about again. "The concubine, of course. Like these lovely creatures. So carefully selected—a type for every taste and desire."

"Why, Colonel Woo?" I asked.

"Why?"

"Yes, why are you offering me your women? We're not exactly old friends, the kind who share bed partners."

Woo chuckled smugly. He bowed and feigned humility again, but his lips were sneering.

"Because Woo has request to make of great American agent."

"Such as?"

"Stop the bombings," he said. "Spare our city further suffering."

"I'm already committed to that. It's my job. You want something more."

"Yes. In time blame will have to be placed. You could do that. You could arrange the evidence."

"To blame whom? The Russians?"

"The Maoists," he said. "The Communist Chinese. Let them bear the blame for this threat against world peace. Do that for me and they are yours . . . one or all of them."

I couldn't keep my eyes from the uneven row of girls, their almost naked bodies glistening in the sun from the huge windows across the room. It would be easy to blame the Chicoms once I tracked down the leadership of the terrorists, and I certainly didn't owe my Red counterparts any loyalty.

"Such a small favor," he said, "for such a delightful reward. What man could refuse, Mr. Carter?"

I hesitated, and in the moment I looked from girl to girl, the door opened. The servant behind me spoke briefly in Chinese, and Colonel Woo stood up irritably.

"Miss Mehta has returned," he said. "We must join her in the dining room."

He came around the desk, smiling again.

"Think about it," he said. "What nights of pleasure you shall have."

At the door I paused. A thought had crossed my mind. I touched Woo on the sleeve, stopping him momentarily.

"There must be more a man of great wealth wants, Colonel Woo. A full belly, all the things he ever wanted, position, all the women his body can use . . . but what else? Surely there must be something more a man like you still craves. What is it, Colonel?"

"Security, Mr. Carter." He laughed. "After all that, a man with everything can lust only for security . . . the ultimate desire and the most elusive."

He went ahead of me into the hall. Holding Chuni's arm, he led her to the massive dining room with its long table and giant chandeliers. He took his place at the end of the table like a reigning sultan.

His answer hadn't satisfied me. Somehow I couldn't imagine him lusting after security. I felt he must want something else. But what?

I had no chance to press the question. Within minutes the long table was filled with wines and foods, a gourmet horn of plenty that spilled out before us.

For a small man Woo put away vast quantities of food and was still eating when the servants brought in a scrawny child from the orphanage down the hill.

An interpreter told us the boy had seen the man called Zakir Shastri only the day before.

I leaned forward, firing questions at the boy in the

clipped staccato that works sometimes in interrogations. But the skinny youngster shrank back from me.

Surprisingly, Chuni came to my rescue.

She spoke to the boy gently in a dialect I hadn't heard before and seemed to win his confidence quickly.

"The man called Shastri frightened him," she told me. "The man offered him food, then tried to coax him into a car. He ran and came here, to Colonel Woo's orphanage."

"Ask him where he saw the man."

Colonel Woo interceded for me. He held out a pheasant leg dripping in red wine sauce and put the question to the boy.

I caught some of the words, enough to know what the boy was saying.

"At the temple with the tower of glowing red," I heard. He said more but I lost the meaning until Chuni translated for me.

"He's not sure," she said. "He remembers only the temple and the guru."

"And the tower of glowing red," Colonel Woo added. "That should help."

Woo smiled and leaned back in his chair proudly. He seemed to think he had solved the entire case for me.

"Most pleased to help American agent," he said as he rose from the table.

He dismissed us almost summarily. He motioned for

his servants, and they led Chuni and me through the
estate and out to the waiting Mercedes.

As we started back toward the city, I pressed her
for information. "I might as well get all I can," I
thought, "before her report to Raj can stop me."

"Many of our temples have towers," she protested.
"Many of them are red. Is it important?"

"Damned important," I told her. "It's the next link
in a chain. Maybe that's where this Shastri hangs out,
sort of his headquarters."

She shook her head, trying to think. "It could be
anywhere. Even an older temple, a ruins . . . the
countryside is dotted with them."

Her answers irritated me. We had wasted hours
with the little colonel, and I was growing impatient.
We reached the center of the city and stopped at the
U.S. consulate, I realized more than ever how rapidly
we were running out of time.

The tension of the city was like static electricity on
a dry day. I could feel it in the air. Dozens of Indian
regular troops stood in front of the consulate, their
rifles on their shoulders. Other troops stretched down
the near side of the grounds.

"You think about that red-towered temple," I told
Chuni. "I'll be inside for just a minute."

I was stopped by a nervous Indian soldier on the
sidewalk. Another soldier questioned me at the steel
gate, then led me to a sergeant at the door. The sergeant asked me some questions, then made a telephone call.

Slocum met me at the door of his office. He wore no tie; his hair was rumpled, and sweat stained his forehead, even though his office was down to sixty-five degrees.

"We're fortifying the building," he said excitedly. "We expect to be hit at any minute."

He walked behind the desk and slumped in his chair. His linen handkerchief came out as he patted the sweat off his wrinkled brow.

"I've asked Washington to send in three hundred combat armed Marines to help protect U.S. life and property," he said.

"Marines!" I snapped.

"For God's sake, we have to match what the Russians do. They're bringing in men already, with New Delhi's blessings."

"You trying to start World War III right here?"

"If that's what the bastards want. . . ."

"That's brilliant."

He gave me a sharp look.

"You haven't heard about the Red fleet?" he asked. "They have a task force that's steaming toward the Bay of Bengal on a training maneuver. Twelve ships led by a missile-launching cruiser."

"You know, you could do it," I said. "You sonsofbitches could keep slapping each other around over here and actually touch off a nuclear war. Why in hell don't you stop and think for once in your goddamned lives?" I was on my feet walking toward his desk. Slocum backed away.

"Have you heard anything more about the fifteenth?" I asked.

"Independence Day? No."

"You said something may be brewing, remember? And I have word that the Russian consulate is going to be blasted. Your offices may get hit at the same time."

Slocum was alert. This affected him.

"You know for sure something might happen then?"

"No. But it's my guess the same people who are planting the bombs are planning something spectacular on August fifteenth. You might consider evacuating the consulate people on the night of the fourteenth."

"Oh, God," he said. "Isn't there something we can do?"

"Sure," I told him. "Tell your guards to keep the kids off the street outside the consulate."

"Kids?"

"Yes. And help me find a temple with a red tower. I need the biggest map of the city you've got."

Slocum pushed his intercom button. Minutes later his secretary was spreading a map of the city on his desk.

Using Colonel Woo's estate as a center point, I drew a circle representing the distance a boy might walk in a matter of hours. Then I called in some of the Indians on Slocum's staff and asked them to pinpoint the temples located inside the circle.

They recalled two with red towers.

"One is a copy of the famous Tower of Victory," an Indian secretary in her fifties told me. "We call it Qutb Minar. It's made of red sandstone and is a hundred feet tall with a circular staircase to the top. It was built before partition. There isn't much of a temple there now."

"And the other one?"

"That would be the Osian temple over at the east side of the city. It's partly in ruins; few people go there."

I thanked her and went out to the car where Chuni waited. When I told her what I had learned, she gave me directions to the first temple the woman had mentioned.

Fifteen minutes later, when we drove up to it, I saw that the Qutb Minar wasn't much of a temple . . . only a tall red tower. I was looking for something else, although I wasn't sure exactly what. Some kind of general headquarters with room for a lot of people —something secluded, hidden, somewhere the authorities wouldn't think of looking.

The Osian temple looked better. Square pillars held up stone arches, facades of fallen buildings, and the courtyard was still a jumble of tumbled stones. At one corner stood a two-story red tower. The ruins extended to one side and into a dense growth of shrubs and trees. Smoke rose through the trees in a gentle spiral.

"I'll have a look."

"I'm coming with you," Chuni insisted.

We walked through the ruins. Sections had been cleared so the faithful could come here to invoke the blessings of their gods.

Partway through the ruins we found a well-worn trail which ran through the edge of the temple ruins and into the undergrowth. We were almost to the trees before I saw the deep green of a large tent.

We stepped quietly off the trail and into the edge of the brush to watch. At first we saw only the trees and the big canvas shelter. Then I spotted a small fire pit outside and a bucket. A man came out of the flap and stretched, looked around, coughed and spat on the ground, then went back inside. We saw no one else. A few wisps of smoke rose from the fire.

Behind us we heard a sound—part sob, part anger, with a touch of hysteria. I turned and saw a figure coming across the trail we had just followed.

It was a man, moving quickly but with a slight limp. As he came closer, I realized he was wide shouldered and powerful, a man who could frighten a child easily. I wondered if this could be Zakir.

We shrank into the brush as he went by. He never looked our way. His breath came in ragged gasps, and I guessed he had been running. I turned to Chuni as soon as he had passed us.

"You go back to the car and wait for me," I told her. "I'm going to follow him."

The path led across the far end of the ruins and through a patch of trees. Soon we were at the back of the old temple. Only one wall remained. Made of heavy block, it was thirty feet high and a hundred feet long. The man leaned against this wall, catching his breath. Then he looked behind him, saw no one and pushed through a thick bush that obviously concealed an opening. He vanished inside.

I gave the man two minutes, then ran to the spot and found the entrance.

It was dark inside. I listened to my own breath rushing in and out of my lungs. There was no other sound. Snapping on my pencil flash, I moved the small beam around. I was in a dirt-walled passageway near a dozen steps that led downward.

At the bottom of the stairs I found candles and American-made matches. A trail of wax on the floor led to the right. The passageway here was taller, seven feet, and had been carved from hard clay, maybe sandstone.

Twenty steps ahead I could see faint light which wavered and flickered. The tunnel smelled incredibly old.

Slowly I edged toward the light. I could hear nothing. The passageway turned sharply. I paused, letting my eyes get used to the new-found light. Ahead was a room twenty feet square, with a ceiling higher than the tunnel. Two passageways led out of the room.

At first I didn't see what made the light. Then I saw torches, fed by some type of oil, blazing in standards, one in the center of each of the four walls. The room was empty.

Moving swifty, I crossed the room to the closest opening and went into the passageway. I paused and looked back. No one seemed to have seen me yet. This tunnel was short, connecting with a larger passage that extended ahead for over two hundred feet before it made a gentle turn. Along the main tunnel, rooms opened up at regular intervals. They seemed to be cells where the monks or priests had meditated, away from the world.

At the far end, the corridor turned again, branched, and became lighter.

Torches lighted the way behind me, but ahead it seemed different. Then I saw the first light bulb hanging from exposed wires.

The tunnel branched here: I went to the right, where the light bulbs were at twenty-foot intervals. A short way ahead the tunnel opened into a large room. The tunnel now narrowed and led into a small balcony along the back of the room.

Below was a frenzy of activity. Fifteen boys, most in their late teens, worked around a table, industriously painting tin cans black. Others cut off lengths of fuse. More boys put the empty cans in boxes and carried them into another room through an archway.

A wave of exhilaration gripped me. I had found the bomb factory or at least one of the plants the terrorists were using to build their fifteen-cent weapons. But there was a chilling effect, too, as I realized the boys here were older than the ones I had seen picking up the potassium nitrate at the chemical plant. They had the look of soldiers. They appeared to know what they were doing, as though they had been trained.

None of them had seen me, but there was no way I could cross the balcony ledge unnoticed. I went back and tried the tunnel to the left. It veered slightly, then kept going in the same general direction as the other branch. Before long it opened into a second series of cell-like rooms. These had been used. Pallets lay in each, with grubby sacks that might have contained the worldly possessions of teen-aged boys.

These tunnels might run for miles under Calcutta. I had to find a way out fast or go back the way I had come. Ahead was another empty room. The room had a desk, some chairs and beyond it a wooden door set into a frame.

No one was in the room. Moving quickly, I ran to the door behind the desk. It was unlocked.

As I opened it, I saw another corridor leading to the surface. I stepped outside and turned back toward the Mercedes.

Chuni wasn't there.

I heard her call to me from the darkness across the the street.

"Nick, over here."

I whirled and some sixth sense clicked inside my skull. Maybe it was a sound or a glint of something metallic in the sunlight. I don't know, but I crouched and dug for my stripped-down Luger.

Then I saw him . . . the big Indian I had tracked into the temple. He was coming at me from the front of the car. He brandished a meat cleaver awkwardly over his head.

Instantly I had my Luger in my hand.

He was no match for the gun, of course, but he kept coming. I fell back, shouting my warning. I didn't want to kill him. I was certain it was Zakir Shastri, and I needed him alive . . . desperately. He sliced the air in front of my face and lashed back again as I retreated.

In desperation I fired, once just inches from his head as a warning and then a second time into his arm. The impact of the high-velocity bullet spun him around, knocking him to the ground; but he got up again and came at me, his arm limp at his side.

I shot him again, this time in the leg. He lurched forward, almost is if he had been thrown.

Instinctively I stepped back, my gun ready for a second assailant, but the only movement I could see was Chuni running across the street toward me.

She flung herself into my arms, but I pushed her away. I could hear the sound of running feet behind us. The boys from inside the temple were pouring out the entrance and scrambling to an old truck at the rear of the ruins.

They were escaping, but I had to check the man on the ground before we could follow them. I rolled him over on his back with my foot.

He was dead. A hole the size of my fist had burst open where his navel had been.

Chuni stood by me, apparently unaffected by the gore. "Who is it?" she asked.

I fished the man's wallet from his pocket and spread it open on the ground. The name on the papers stood out boldly.

"Zakir Shastri." I'd found him at last.

I knelt beside the body. I immediately spotted the bloody holes in the man's arm and leg. I hadn't missed.

Somebody else had shot him in the back. The slug had come out the front, pushing his navel ahead of it like a blooming flower.

Someone wanted Shastri dead before he could talk, someone who had stood across the street as the big Indian made his suicidal attack with his knife.

But who?

CHAPTER X

"Look!" Chuni shouted.

I rose from the dead man and looked back toward the truck. Loaded with boys, it was careening into the street, picking up speed. It swerved to miss a sacred cow that lay in the gutter, then drove a path straight through the small crowd of people who were coming out of their houses in response to the gunshots. The people scrambled for the edge of the street and the truck skidded around the corner.

"Come on," I yelled at Chuni. "We'll follow it."

The window behind my head popped and crackled as we jumped into the Mercedes. The slug left a spider-web effect that filled the entire pane. Another bullet thumped into the door and ended up somewhere in the seat underneath me.

Obviously Shastri wasn't the only intended target, but right now I couldn't take the time to fight back.

I gunned the engine and the Mercedes leaped ahead like a jackrabbit. We nearly rolled at the corner, and Chuni screamed as she tried to brace herself.

We jumped the curb, ran a hundred feet along the sidewalk and finally got back into the street. I could still see the truck lumbering ahead of us, so I slowed down and let another vehicle get in front of us for cover.

"Are you hurt?" I asked Chuni.

She peered up at me and shook her head. She kept looking out the back window, but there was no tail. She was scared.

"Keep your eyes on the truck," I ordered. "If we lose that, we start all over again."

Remaining a block behind, we followed the slowly moving truck deeper into the city. A half hour later it stopped near the side entrance of Dum Dum Airport and disgorged the teen-aged boys. The driver, a skinny Indian in Western dress, herded them into the terminal.

We left the Mercedes and followed them out to the flight line. An old DC-3 that looked as if it had flown the hump into Burma way back in World War II waited for them.

As they boarded, I swore to myself. Tailing an airplane wasn't an easy stunt.

"Can you get us their flight plan?" I asked Chuni. "Maybe Raj can help you."

She thought about it a moment before she disappeared toward the stairway to the flight control tower. The DC-3 was already at the end of the runway by the time she came back.

She beamed happily and swung a set of keys in front of me. "They're headed for Raxaul," she said. "In the slopes to the Himalayas, near Nepal. About five hundred miles from here."

"Did you get us a plane too?" I asked.

"A Piper Comanche," she replied. "Ever flown one?"

"Yes."

"So have I." She took my hand and led me out of the terminal.

"It'll be dark," I protested. "Are you sure there's a lighted field?"

She laughed. "Don't worry. We'll drop matches to illuminate the runway."

I hesitated, but she ran ahead of me to the hangar. By the time I reached it, she had spoken to the uniformed cop outside and was shouting orders to the mechanics. They rolled out the Comanche and we boarded her. Ten minutes later we took off and banked northward.

It was a long flight, and it was dark before we spotted the lights of the village. She radioed ahead and someone below illuminated the field with vehicle lights. Chuni circled once before she dropped the plane confidently to the hard-packed dirt of the air strip. Only two other aircraft were on the ground, one of them the DC-3 we had seen take off in Calcutta.

Chuni taxied to the tie-down area, and we roped the plane to the ground, wing and tail, before we checked out the DC-3. It was empty. There was no sign of the crew or of the boys we had seen board it in Calcutta.

At the small terminal building a single man sat behind the counter, a government official. He seemed bored until Chuni showed him a card from her wallet. Then he brightened and brought out the teapot. As we sipped the weak brew, he told us the planeload of boys had landed an hour ahead of us and a truck had picked them up.

That was all he knew. He showed us to a back room where we could rest until morning.

With the first light of day we started down the dirt road to the village.

I didn't like the looks of the town. A few stone houses, desolate, wind-swept foothills, one street with a few scrawny trees struggling in the sparse soil, and dust everywhere. The dirt road was hard packed and showed the recent passage of a truck. I saw one other motor vehicle in the area, an old Rambler, which looked strange and out of place high in the Himalayan foothills.

Chuni talked to the man who owned the Rambler. "We need your car to go exploring," she said. "There's so much we can't see from the air. We can pay you well."

The man wasn't interested. He told us the car wouldn't run and turned back to the stone he was chipping.

At another house we stopped to ask if the occupants had seen the truck loaded with boys. The woman listened patiently at first. Then something Chuni said made her angry. Her eyes flared and she slammed the door.

Chuni was upset. "People just don't do that in India," she said. "We listen, we disagree, and we smile all the time. That woman was scared. I don't like it."

At the next house we got a similar refusal, but it was tempered. The old man there seemed immune to fear. He was too close to the grave already.

"No one will tell of the truck," he said. "We have seen it before with its load of young. But those who ask too many questions don't last long. Go back to Calcutta. There is only death here. Even speaking with you will make my family suspect. Go home."

He backed away, closing the door behind him.

Chuni's face wrinkled in a puzzled frown. "Perhaps we should go back," she said. "We are bringing trouble to these people. They have enough without us."

"You mean just forget the trouble brewing in Calcutta?"

"No, but we could tell Raj. He could send in the army if necessary."

I told her "no" and continued to follow the tracks left by the truck. She hesitated only a moment before she caught up with me. She didn't protest again as we walked through the village and followed the curving trail of the truck tires toward the upward slopes.

Behind us the village was coming alive. The peasants were emerging from their hovels, watching us curiously. Obviously, strangers, at least Westerners, were a rarity in that area. I wondered if word would spread ahead of us that we were here.

We walked two miles up the incline and rested at the first sign of some brush. We were in a small ravine. I stood looking up at the mountains with their year-around cap of sparkling snow.

"It's hopeless," I said, more to myself than to Chuni. "What?" she asked.

I waved my hand toward the mountains and then took in the sprawling valley below.

"We don't even know what we're looking for. The mountains stretch for hundreds of miles. That truck could have been heading anywhere. We haven't a chance of keeping up on foot."

"We can go back then?" she said hopefully.

I ignored her. Time was my enemy now. If we went back, we would lose an entire day. The fifteenth was coming up too quickly.

I scanned the horizon again, picking out small segments at a time, concentrating carefully, then moving my eyes to the next patch of landscape. Finally I saw it . . . a faint movement in the brush three hundred yards ahead of us.

We were being watched. That was a good sign. But whoever we were searching for could still stay out of sight easily in the scrub brush that grew all over the foothills, and an army could hide in the ravines and draws that ran upward to meet the mountains.

We had no chance of finding the truck or the boys it had hauled if they cared to stay out of sight. Whoever we were looking for would have to come to us. It was our only hope.

So I pulled the Luger from the holster and aimed it in the general direction of the movement I had seen on the horizon.

Chuni gasped. "What are you doing? Are you crazy?"

"I'm trying to get captured," I said.

"Captured?"

"By the people in the truck." I pulled the trigger and the gun barked once. "You'd better get back to the plane," I told her. "Fly to Calcutta. Get help."

I pulled the trigger again.

"No," she protested. She pulled my hand down and stopped me from firing again. "You'll be killed."

"Go back," I insisted, but she wouldn't move.

I put the Luger away and took her in my arms. Her body quivered against me.

"Maybe I can help," she said. "I'm trained, you know."

I started to push her away from me, but it was too late. Almost before we heard the sound of the engine, a small truck came rocketing down the roadway from the mountains.

Four men, all wearing army-style web belts and

carrying rifles, leaped out. All four muzzles leveled at me.

"Hey, what's going on?" I demanded indignantly. "Why the guns?"

A tall, lean Indian man with a turban got out of truck and came to look at us.

"You were shooting," he said in Hindi, then again in perfect English.

"A snake," I lied. "A cobra. It scared my wife."

He ignored the lie and studied Chuni carefully. "You fly that red airplane down in the village?" he asked.

I nodded.

"Why did you stop here? We are far from the tourist routes."

"Sightseeing. This is the first time I've been to India."

The man in the turban glanced at Chuni dubiously, and I thought fast.

"I met my wife at the United Nations in New York," I explained.

He didn't believe me, but he continued the charade for a minute more.

"Would you like to ride with us?" he asked politely.

"Yes," Chuni agreed. "I'm quite tired."

Graciously the man walked ahead of us and helped Chuni into the front seat. I climbed in beside her and watched as the armed men got in the back.

The motor rumbled into action, and for the slightest fraction of a second I caught the glimpse of a rifle butt in the rearview mirror. It was coming down hard on my skull. There was only time to move slightly to the left. The blow was a glancing one, but still the heavy wooden stock caught me squarely enough to jar my brains with the stunning impact. I felt that sick sensation that comes just before unconsciouness sweeps its gentle cover of velvet over the mind.

Later, when I groaned and sat up, I found I was tied hand and foot. My hands were in front of me, and two of the para-military men who watched me had their pistols trained on my belly.

I didn't know how far we had come, but I couldn't have been knocked out for more than twenty minutes. Before I could wonder anything else, the truck slowed and crept through a gate. On each side were double rolls of concertina barbed wire and a double apron fence of wire.

The tall man came to the back of the truck.

"Cut the cords on his feet and take him to my office," he said.

"Hey!" I spit out with mock anger. "What's the big idea slugging me and tying me up?"

One of the soldiers hit me on the face with the back of his hand. The others laughed.

They pushed me ahead of them, and I could hear Chuni behind us. She was using strictly unladylike language on the two armed men who were half carrying her in the other direction.

They were a ragtag bunch, in spite of the military

overtones. The soldiers in the truck pushed and shoved me as I walked between them toward a low building to the left, which had a door but no windows. A single lamp added to the light that came in around the door. I was pushed inside, and the door closed quickly behind me.

The room was an office of sorts with a filing cabinet, a desk and a typewriter.

"Your papers say your name is Matson, Howard Matson," he said. "I want to know the truth. Who are you, and why are you snooping around here?"

"I'm a businessman, that's all."

"Carrying these?" he asked. He held up Wilhelmina and Hugo. Evidently they had taken them from me in the truck. He put them aside and turned back to me with a ghoulish grin on his face. "Really, Mr. Matson, you underestimate us."

I decided to play the role of self-important American a little longer, although I suspected my captors might know more about me than they were ready to admit.

"Look, you," I snapped. "You might be a big shot to these stupid Indian peasants, but to me you're just another hoodlum pushing people around. You and your mercenary boy scouts look like hell. I've seen better discipline in a pack of wolves. You start pushing me and you'll get shoved back so hard it'll make your teeth rattle. Now untie my hands!"

It was the old cold-shower technique, and it served its purpose. It rattled him, made him angry. He stood up and slapped me hard; I spun away, and as I turned, kicked him viciously. He cried out. Then somebody hit me in the kidneys from behind. The pain was excruciating.

I quit fighting and let two of them pull me to a table. They cut the ropes that bound me and held guns at my head.

"Strip," their leader ordered. "Naked."

I didn't argue. When my clothes were laid aside, they pulled me roughly to the table and tied me there, spread-eagle.

Their leader limped over to the table and sneered down at me with tobacco-stained teeth.

"Now, Mr. Matson," he began. "Perhaps you would like to tell us about yourself. Who are you? What are you doing here?"

"I'm an American," I said boldly. "That's all you need to know. By the time the American consul hears of this. . . ."

He laughed. So did the men around him.

"The consul? In Calcutta? You must be joking, Mr. Matson, or whatever your name is. In two days there will be no American consulate in Calcutta. Perhaps no Calcutta. But you know all that, don't you?"

I said I didn't know what he was talking about. He nodded with exaggerated patience.

"Of course, of course," he said, turning away.

When he faced me again, I could see a straight razor in his hand. Suddenly I was certain getting captured hadn't been such a good idea, after all.

"Have you ever felt pain, Matson?" the man asked. "Excruciating, unbearable pain that tears your insides out and starts you screaming for a quick death?"

The razor came past my face; it was six inches long, hinged and honed to a sharpness that made it glint softly in the morning light. When it first touched my skin I didn't think it was cutting—the slice was so controlled, so smooth. I turned my head to look at my left hand. The blade had started at the very tip of my index finger, sliced down through my palm, continued across my wrist and straight to my shoulder, then turned until it stopped just over my collar bone.

The first pain seeped through as I saw the blade slicing my wrist. I closed my eyes, but the pattern was set. I wanted to scream.

"Have you heard of the death of a thousand slashes, Mr. Matson? It's an old Oriental torture, usually used when information is desired and the life of the subject is of no importance. Oh, I won't say all victims of a thousand slices die. A few have survived. Their bodies are one continuous mass of scar tissue. Notice how the slices begin just through the first layer of skin so only a few drops of blood form along the line. As we continue, they will find other paths and go deeper and deeper. When the slashes leave the head and chest and move down to the pubic region, the strongest men scream. Few men can endure the pain."

The next slash was the same as the first, but on my right arm and hand. The blade went deeper this time . . . a searing, burning drumroll of pain that drew an involuntary snort of surprise from my nostrils. My teeth and lips were clamped shut. I thought, "If I refuse to open my mouth, it'll be easier to keep my screams of pain inside."

The tall man knew his work. I could see a gleam of pleasure in his eye, a slow tightening around his nose and the curl of his lips as the blade moved once again to my body—this time at my chin—and traced another line down my chest to my belly.

The Indian was talking again. I blinked open my eyes, not knowing when I had closed them.

"The tolerance of pain is interesting. Some Westerners fall completely to pieces at this point. With the first slice they tell everything they know. With the second slash they are weeping and crying for mercy. On the third slice they go into hysterics or faint. Your tolerance of pain, or your training, is much better than I would have imagined." He finished the slicing.

"Now, the questions. Who sent you to spy on us?"

I kept quiet. I had to think about a way out, some escape. For the moment it looked hopeless. The knots were good ones; I knew from trying to stretch them that there was no give at either my hands or feet. The table was narrow and easily tipped, but even if I rolled and tossed, there still was little I could do.

"Who sent you to spy on us, Matson?"

The knife came again a quarter of an inch from the other mark on my arm. It cut deeper still, drawing a gasp of shock from me.

The door opened. A soldier pushed his head in.

"Fire!" he yelled. His face registered excitement and he shouted the warning again. "Fire, Captain! Out there."

The leader scowled. He appeared disappointed at the interruption as he laid the razor aside.

"Don't run away, Matson," he said.

He and the guards darted through the door and I breathed a sigh of relief. I had no idea what was happening outside, but I welcomed the interruption.

I wanted to close my eyes against the pain or cry out for help, but both ideas were useless. I didn't have a minute to waste.

I looked around the room. At first I couldn't see any way out, no way to free myself from the ropes that were biting into my flesh. Then I thought of the kerosene lamp that burned on the desk nearby.

The more I looked at the lamp, the faster the idea grew. It was a gamble, but the odds were better than if I waited for the captain to come back with his deadly little razor. If only I could topple the lamp and get the flames to the ropes around my wrists, I stood a chance.

But getting to it wasn't easy. I could barely move. By bouncing and squirming, I could only make the table tip a little. It took all my strength to roll and toss enough to make it wobble. But it finally tipped and fell over on its side. The fall stunned me and added to my agony.

Judging the distance to the desk, I slowly inched the table to the right. Then I rolled over on my belly,

pulling the table on top of me and using it as a batter-
ing ram against the desk. The lamp wavered, then fell.
It broke on the floor and whooshed into a puddle of
oily flames.

Fortunately it wasn't too full, but I still had to work
fast before the kerosene soaked into the dirt of the
floor.

It took all my strength to roll on my side far enough
to get my hands above the flames where the fire could
eat slowly into the stout cords that bound me.

It soon began to burn my wrist too. I jerked hard
with my right hand to pull it away from the flames.
The cord kept burning.

Pain started to billow into my brain. The cord
burned and I could see it singe the hair on my wrist,
then redden the flesh. Again I jerked my right arm;
the rope cut into my wrist painfully. Once more I
yanked, and the wrist came free.

I tore the rest of the rope from my hand, then pulled
at the knots on my left arm. They were well tied. My
whole right hand and wrist screamed with pain from
the fire. But this was my only chance to get out. At
last the knots came loose; I tore off the cords around
my feet and found my clothes. My pistol and knife lay
on the desk top. I dressed, slid into my shoes and was
ready to go when the tall Indian came through the
door. He looked pretty unhappy when he saw me with
my gun aimed at his stomach.

He stared at it, expecting me to shoot him. In fact,
he was so intent on the gun he hardly saw the blade

of the knife in my other hand. It entered his body just above his groin.

A gurgling sound came from his lips as he backed off the knife and cupped his hands over the wound. Then he melted to the floor.

He wasn't dead when I rolled him over.

"Where's the girl?" I asked.

"Gone," he said. Blood came out the side of his mouth and he gagged. "She set fire to her room. Please .... Help me. I ...."

Then suddenly he was gone, a corpse at my feet.

I was sorry. I would have preferred to keep him alive, but a knife is not an accurate weapon.

I looked around the room. An automatic rifle rested in one corner and there were two hand grenades on a shelf. I pocketed the grenades and held the rifle ready as I went to the door. I had to find out what was going on here that was tied in with Calcutta, and I had to find Chuni. I eased open the door and stepped outside.

CHAPTER XI

I went out cautiously. I had found a quilted jacket inside, so I felt more like part of the scene. With my head down, I might pass briefly for one of the guards.

I could smell the smoke from the fire and hear the shouts of men battling the flames that spit from a grass-roofed shack.

I had entered a courtyard surrounded by one-story buildings that gave the impression of a fort from the old American West. There were a dozen buildings, three of them like barracks and another apparently a mess hall. Three trucks sat in front of one structure.

Only the excitement over the fire kept the attention of a dozen uniformed men away from me as I hurried in the direction of the trucks. I had almost reached them when a man appeared from behind the nearest vehicle. He walked directly in front of me, holding his hand up as a warning. He looked at me curiously, then backed away and seemed about to shout for help when I called to him. Surprised, he came over, his face suspicious.

"Make one noise and you're a dead man," I said. "Now turn and walk beside me. I've got a gun pointing at you." I spoke to him rapidly in Hindi, hoping he understood it and not one of the other dialects that divided the country.

He turned, the fear on his face so strong that I could almost smell it. We walked two hundred yards before we topped the rise and went down the other side. When we were out of sight of the camp, I pushed him to the ground.

"Did you see the girl?" He nodded. "Which way did she go?"

He pointed up the slope we were on.

"Who runs this place?" I asked.

"I don't know," he said, his voice trembling with fear. "I am only Naga, the cook. I don't know."

"Okay." I motioned with the rifle for him to get up. "Show me where the girl went."

He led me quickly up the slope and to the west. We came out on a ridge surrounding a small valley. I saw a dozen houses below, some half burned, others completely demolished. We watched for five minutes without seeing any movement below. He pointed past some brush to another place a quarter of a mile around the ridge.

"That is where the command post is. If your lady got this far, she is probably hiding below, waiting for darkness."

We melted from stone to bush, from rock to tree. When we were two hundred yards away, Naga held up his hand. We could hear someone talking. Another cautious fifty yards and we saw them. The command post was twenty feet downslope from the lip of the ridge.

We checked the surrounding area, but there didn't seem to be any security men out. Silently we crawled closer until we were on the ridge directly above them. I pulled the pin on the first hand grenade, then checked the target again.

Six men stood in a pillbox dug deep into the side of the cliff. Two had automatic rifles. Another was setting up a small radio. One had field glasses trained on the village.

The grenade bounced into the command post. Then the rifle was at my shoulder, jerking and rattling as my slugs slammed into the men. The explosion came as an anticlimax. Two of the men were already down. The grenade blew the rest of them into a writhing, bleeding mass. We didn't wait to see if anyone survived. We ran down the hall, around the post and on toward the buildings a quarter of a mile below. I saw Chuni then, hiding among the rocks. Four men below had been moving closer to her as they searched the area, but at the sound of the grenade and the slugs from my automatic, they had panicked and fallen back.

She saw us coming and ran to meet us.

I caught her in my arms and carried her. Part of her hair had been singed, and her face was black with soot.

"Don't take me back to the village," she said, trembling.

I stopped. "It's protection."

"No, it's . . . it's too gruesome. They don't bury anyone. They just shoot them and leave them there. Women and children and old men. . . ."

I turned and looked at Naga. He nodded.

"It is true. They train their men with real people. . . ."

"Stay here with her," I told Naga. "I've got to take a look at that place."

I took off at a trot and smelled the rotting, bloated flesh before I went twenty yards. A dozen buzzards flew up when I rounded the first house. The partial remains of an old man and a boy lay in the street.

Walls of the buildings were pocked with shells and bullets. Most of the houses were rock and mortar, showing hundreds of bullet holes.

Around the next house I saw three women. One of the bodies had the breasts cut off; a second one had lost its head. At the last house a man had been nailed to the door upside down, then shot at close range.

I ran back, not looking at either side along the shell-pitted street. There would be a massacre if these guerrillas ever entered Calcutta.

When I got back to the spot where I had left Chuni, I found only Naga, crumpled on the ground. I couldn't help him. He had died hard, his bowels ripped out and his throat slashed. There was no sign of the girl.

If they had her, then they must be close by. . . .

The sudden chatter of a machine gun erupted, placing a row of bullets in the ground six feet to my right. I turned, but no one was there. Another chattering of the gun and slugs ripped into the ground at my left. I rolled toward a tree, firing blindly to keep their heads down, but still I saw no one. I was utterly exposed. For them it was like shooting sharks in a goldfish pond.

"Really, Mr. Carter, there is no need to struggle," a voice called to me. "You are completely surrounded, hopelessly outgunned. You are too smart a man to try to break out of this. Why not just throw down your gun and come in quietly."

The powerful, convincing voice came from a bull horn that seemed to echo from every side of the small valley.

I threw down the rifle and stood, putting my hands over my head. Four "rocks" on the hill in front of me rose, discarded their camouflage and came toward me at a trot, their automatic rifles aimed at my chest.

The Indian guerrillas were all around me, stripping me of Hugo and Wilhelmina. Then they pushed me roughly ahead.

We didn't go back to the camp. The guards swung me high around it, where we hit another road. Half a mile beyond the rise we came to a small canyon. Three sides were steeply cut, as if an old rock quarry had been operated there at one time. At the rear was a large cave. Over the entrance to the cave had been woven a heavy barbed-wire gate.

The guards marched me up to the gate. They unwired and unlocked a small section of it, shoved me through, and closed the gate at once. I saw about thirty people—some sick, some crying, all ill-clothed and apparently unfed. I turned back to the gate and a well-dressed man in a bright green uniform with bars on the shoulder came up. He looked into the compound.

"Mr. Carter. Come forward, please."

I went up to the barbed wire.

"News came from Calcutta," he said, peering at me curiously through his glasses. "We just learned the name of our distinguished guest. I have heard much about you. The man no one can kill. We may go down in history."

I ignored his jibes. "What's going to happen on August fifteenth?" I demanded. "That's the big date, isn't it?"

He scowled. "Nothing you'll be around to see."

He turned away, then thought of something. "Don't worry about the girl," he said. "She'll be with you in the village."

When he was gone, I tried to gather my thoughts. Obviously, he wasn't the leader. The man I had to find would be safe in the city, masterminding the final arrangements.

I had to get to that man. But first I had to stay alive, and at the moment that alone looked difficult enough.

I examined the cave. The fence across the entrance was electrified, probably with enough juice to fry me, and the walls were forty feet of rock. A man could spend a lifetime digging through them. Escape seemed impossible.

I wasn't alone, but the people who shared my predicament wouldn't be much help. Most of them were old and feeble, probably peasants who scratched a living from the cruel soil of the mountain foothills. They were preparing for death as stolidly as only a Hindu can. Sitting cross-legged on the dirt floor of the cave, their heads bowed, they repeatedly chanted their prayer to the gods: *"Hare Krishna, Hare Rama."*

They were ready for the next step in the long cycle of reincarnation. But I wasn't.

I went among them, trying to rouse them from their stupor of fatality, but none of them appeared to notice me. Only when I came to a young man leaning against the wall did I get a reaction.

He laughed when he saw me. "So, they caught a big fish in the net. You're English?"

"American," I told him.

"Welcome. By noon we'll all be dead."

I knelt beside him and held out a cigarette. He took it and gagged on the smoke.

"What about you?" I asked. "How come they plan to kill you? The others are old. Why don't they want you with them?"

"I was," he said. "They recruited me in Calcutta. They fed me and cared for my sister. Then I saw the village here. I could not kill like that, so they put me in here with the untouchables, the lepers and the widows chanting for the souls of their husbands." He stopped and glared at the guard. "Soon they will come and pick out four or five and drive us to the village. If we don't move fast enough, we'll be bayonetted or shot. I've seen them do it before."

The young man was shaking with fear and anger.

"Do you know what they're planning?" I asked. "Anything they want to do on Independence Day? Have you heard about it?"

His brown eyes darted at me like the tongue of a cobra. "Of course, but how do you know about that? They told us, but you're from the outside." He shrugged and sat on his haunches, staring at the ground. "The great revolution. We were going to take over Calcutta and all of West Bengal if we could. They told us they had the police on their side; the Americans and Russians would be shooting at each other. All we had to do was blow up the Howrah Bridge and the railway station, then sweep down Chowringhi Road burning every building to the ground. Calcutta would be in such a panic we could move in with a hundred men and command the whole state."

"Will it work?" I asked.

The young man shook his head. "I don't know. For months they've been training men. The Calcutta Liberation Army, they call it. When the consulates blow up, that will be the signal. Small squads will strike at key facilities. It might work." He shrugged.

"For us it won't matter," he continued. "Every morning they have war games in the village. They always take the strongest ones to provide sport for the trainees. Besides, they had to dispose of the people in the town below to keep them quiet."

I was on my feet walking along the wall, squinting into the dark corners of the cave. "Is there any way out of here?"

His head moved slightly indicating a "no."

I checked my pockets, but there was nothing left, only my belt. The garroting wires would do me no good now. I had matches there too, but nothing in the damp cave would burn.

It had to be the village. There we would have some freedom, some chance. I looked back at the crumpled heap that had once been a young man.

"What will it be like in the village when we get there?"

He laughed, a hollow, mocking laugh.

"There is no reason to fight the inevitable. Simply relax and pray for something better in the life ahead."

I bent and grabbed the man, jerking him to his feet, pushing him hard against the damp cave wall.

"You've got to tell me exactly what happens in the village. If you've seen it, tell me what the men with the guns do, where the victims go."

I relaxed my grip on his arm. His eyes stabbed at me, alert now, fearful, angered.

"They will take five or six, march us to the top of the ridge, then release us, firing into the ground, forcing us to run into the village. There are seventeen houses, huts and small buildings. We will try to hide in them. If it's the regulars, they'll work smoothly, flushing us out, firing near us or perhaps hitting our legs so we can go on to another house to hide. When the last house is flushed out, they will shoot us or bayonet us for practice. The teen-age recruits are the worst. They bet to see how long each victim lives."

I shook my head. "What weapons will they have?"

"Rifles, automatic rifles, hand grenades and long knives."

I started to lean against the damp wall when I saw movement at the head of the cave near the wire gate.

"They're coming," the young man said.

"What's your name?" I asked.

"Call me Joe—a good American name."

I moved away from him and stood against the wall, waiting. Two guards came in, followed by four young men in civilian clothes. All had automatic weapons. The largest guard looked at me and motioned.

"Outside!" he shouted. "You will be first!"

I moved slowly; the point of a bayonet jabbed painfully into my buttocks. Another guard lifted Joe and pushed him toward the door. The light blinded me as I went through the opening in the gate.

With my eyes narrowed to slits, I saw five people near me. Joe was one. There were three women and one old man, who was large but wasted. The old man left the cave, then turned toward the sun and sat down on the ground.

"Up!" the guards yelled. He ignored them.

A bayonet jabbed into his arm, but he didn't move.

The blade stabbed through the muscle of his upper arm. Only then did he scream. The guard nodded and the four teen-agers with automatic weapons took out knives and plunged toward the old man.

The blades rose and sliced, jabbed and drove in deeply, until the old frame tipped and he fell flat on his back. Still the knives flashed in the soft sunlight, their blades now sticky red. The man made no other sound, only a soft bubble as the last breath gushed from his bloody lips.

"Enough," the guard said. He spoke to the remaining five of us. "You will walk quickly. You will not get out of line or you will die on the spot. You will keep up with the guards."

The young men wiped their knives clean on the dead old man's trousers, then marshaled us into a line. Two of the teen-agers were in front and two in back.

The walk to the village was too quick; I still hadn't thought of a plan to help us. It went exactly as Joe said it would. At the top of the ridge they told us to run for the buildings. As I looked down, I caught sight of a lonely figure part way down the slope. It was Chuni.

I slammed down the slope as fast as I could, hoping not to catch a bullet in the back.

"Run," I called as I reached her.

We ducked behind a stone wall, and I felt safer for the moment. Joe slid in beside us. I took off my belt, whipped out one of the thin garroting wires, concealed there and handed it to him.

"If you get a chance, use this on one of them."

He frowned, then smiled, and I thought I saw a gleam of hope in his eyes.

Before I could think of anything else, two brown bodies hurtled around the corner of the building. They were boys no more than thirteen. Each held a rifle. First one fired, then the other, and I could hear the hot lead slap past my head as we ran.

I found a door and ducked inside, pulling Chuni with me. It was the largest building in the village, with a crude loft across one end. The loft was about ten feet wide, enough to hide on for a moment. We climbed up the pole ladder at one side and onto the thick pine boards. A small wooden box rested on the floor. I pushed Chuni to the far wall and motioned for her to lie down.

I had been wondering if the young hunters would have grenades. A moment later I knew. The small bomb came through the window below us, bounced once, then exploded a foot off the floor. There was no time to duck. Part of my body was exposed to the spray of shrapnel but I felt no hot steel. As the smoke cleared, a young boy came into the room cautiously. Holding an automatic short-barreled chattergun, he scanned the room quickly, then made a closer search. Just as he looked at the loft, I threw the wooden box.

He had no time to move. The box smashed the weapon from his hands and jammed one corner into his stomach. He spun in a half circle, grabbed his stomach and crumpled to the floor, the wind knocked from him. I watched the burp gun. It could be our ticket out of there. But just as I started to get it, another boy ran into the room. He saw his buddy on the floor, squinted suspiciously at the loft and sprayed it from below with bullets from his chopper. His aim and the two inches of solid pine saved us.

A moment later he had dragged the unconscious boy out of the room, and the rifle went with him.

I went down the ladder, and Chuni followed. A hand-sized chunk of stone lay on the floor. That would have to do. I threw it out the door in one quick motion, then flattened myself against the wall and waited. The rock struck some metal on the next building and at once I heard a rattle of rifle fire. Steps pounded our way. I tried to time it perfectly. At the last moment I lunged out the door and caught the boy soldier in full gait. I muffled his mouth in one hand and dragged him inside.

I tied his hands and feet with strips from his shirt while Chuni put a gag over his mouth. The rifle he carried looked workable but when I tried to put a round into the chamber, I found it was jammed.

Blindly, we left the doorway and headed back the way the boy had come.

A noise behind me made me spin around, the rifle cocked and ready, but my finger eased on the trigger as Joe hit the ground with the butt of a rifle and squirmed up beside us.

There was anger on his face. "I got one of them with the garrote; at least I got one."

"You ready to go up the hill?"

Joe nodded.

As we rounded the first wall, Chuni tugged at my sleeve, her face death-white. One of the women who came with us lay on her back, her stomach ripped open, her chest a mass of blood; her heart rested in one of her open hands.

I pulled Chuni past the woman and ran for the next building. We heard more firing and screaming behind us.

We ran over a bloated corpse. The face had been eaten away by vultures. We paused behind a wall, covered from both front and back now, and began panting to catch our breath. Chuni looked exhausted.

She took the rifle from me, worked at the trigger guard then the breach for a moment, and I heard the round click into place and slide into the chamber. She gave the rifle back to me with a sigh.

Carefully I looked around the wall from ground level. No one was in front of us. The slope of the hill we had run down minutes before slanted upward three hundred yards before it topped the ridge. It was a long run with no cover. I wasn't sure if Chuni could make it, but she said she was ready.

We jumped up and scurried around the wall, ready to charge up the rise ahead of us. We didn't get there.

Chuni ran head-on into a small boy with a long gun. Her hand flew out instinctively with a karate chop to the neck, and the boy went down, unconscious before he tumbled to the blood-soaked ground. Chuni caught his weapon.

Behind him was one of the guards who had brought us. He had the chatter gun aimed at us.

"Turn around," he said.

I shot him so quickly he never even saw me move the rifle. The bullet went into his chest, slamming him back six feet into the red dust. We ran again.

We were only halfway up the hill when bullets started hitting the ground all around us. The guns from below were being used with precision. We dodged and ran, dodged and changed direction, but kept moving upward.

Ten yards from the top a form rose with an automatic rifle, spraying lead toward us. Joe shot at him but missed. Again my rifle rose and fired; the man spun and sprawled toward us down the hill. We ran past him and over the top.

The man who sat in the jeep was more surprised than we were. The camp commander, the one in the snappy green uniform, had just lowered a brown bottle and was wiping his lips. I shot the bottle out of his hands.

He raised his hands above his head, all of the bravado gone now that the guns were pointed at him.

I ran forward and searched him, finding what I had missed most during these last few minutes of action . . . Hugo and Wilhelmina. It felt good to have them back. I turned to the commander.

"Out!" I ordered him sharply.

He appeared confused.

"Get out of the jeep," I roared at him. He jumped out and stood in front of me, quivering. "Take off your jacket and your shirt." He frowned but did as I ordered.

I took his glasses and threw them into the rocks.

"Over the side, Commandant. Down into the village."

"No, you can't!" he screamed. "They won't recognize me without the uniform. . . ."

I knocked him down with my fist. My foot slammed into him before the white hot surge of hatred melted from me. I gave Chuni the rifle, jerked the man to his feet and threw him over the edge of the ridge. He rolled part way, then Joe and I fired bullets beside him and in back of him until he ran in terror down into the hell of his own creation.

As he entered the first row of houses, we heard the chatter of rifles and automatic weapons fire.

I put Chuni in the jeep. Joe sat in back and traded his rifle for the commandant's automatic. We drove down the bumpy trail toward the camp. I figured there would be few men on duty, since most of the crew would be in Calcutta waiting for the signal to take over the city.

Chuni took the rifle as we approached the first building. I shifted into second, tromped on the gas and skidded around the first corner. The four men who were standing there with mess kits scattered as we slammed past them. Ahead were two trucks. I pointed at them and Joe shot out two tires on each one as we careered past, around the corner and down through the barbed wire gate.

"Think the plane will still be there?" I asked.

Chuni nodded. "I heard the commander tell someone he would fly back to Calcutta after dark."

I grunted. Then the little plane should be gassed and ready to go. But would they have security at the field? I guessed they wouldn't.

We drove right to the field and Chuni checked with the manager, telling him we were taking off at once. He was frowning as the three of us got into the plane and began to taxi toward the end of the field.

I should have known what was happening as soon as I noticed the jeep moving. It came toward us, angling onto the runway and stopping two hundred yards from our position.

Chuni nodded when she saw the vehicle. She revved up the engines, let them warm and then moved down the runway directly at the jeep. We charged down the field; the man in the jeep jumped out and ran for cover. I wanted to grab the controls, to swerve the plane. Chuni's teeth dug into her lower lip as she jockeyed the rudder pedals, keeping the nose of the plane dead on the center of the runway and the jeep.

At the last possible moment she pulled back hard on the wheel. The little plane seemed genuinely surprised at the request but did its best. It leaped up on the sudden rush of air over the control surfaces . . . then I could almost hear the plane sigh; there wasn't enough forward speed for that sort of thing yet. The plane settled back to the runway. But we had hopped over the jeep and were now screaming down the runway for a normal takeoff. I thought I heard one rifle shot, but it didn't seem to do any damage.

I settled back in my seat as we finally took off, feeling the aches and burns of the past few hours. My wrist was throbbing from the searing of the flames. The slices on my arms and chest stung from the salty sweat, and I was so tired I wanted to sleep for a year.

"We'll never make Calcutta," Chuni said, pointing at the fuel gauge.

"Put down at the nearest field," I told her. "We'll rest tonight, refuel and go on to the city tomorrow."

She sighed with relief and leaned over to check the charts.

CHAPTER XII

We flew lower the next day as we passed over the Ganges, the great river of faith of the Hindu religion. The Ganges has many outlets; one of them is the Hooghly River that runs through Calcutta. We turned south to follow the great river toward the city.

Suddenly something came at us looking like a black dot on the horizon. At first I thought it must be a sea-gull, but a tenth of a second later I realized it was a jet fighter smashing through the air over the Comanche at twice the speed of sound. The Comanche went into a violent power-on stall, then half a twist of a spin, while Chuni fought with the controls to pull the nose up. The air felt like the middle of a thunderstorm as the turbulence of the screaming jet flowed over us.

Joe cowered beside me, his nostrils wide with fright as the plane threatened to rip apart.

Two more of the black dots appeared on the horizon. Chuni put the Comanche into a dive, getting down as close to the trees as she dared.

Watching the jets go overhead, I could see the large

red stars and the swept-wing configuration of MIG 23s. These were the best the Russians had.

Chuni pointed behind and above us at a medium Russian bomber. Frisking around the mother ship were six more of the swept-wing fighters.

"Looks like the Reds are moving in with force," I said.

Chuni turned on the airport frequency and listened. Almost at once the air was filled with Russian and English. Both groups were trying to get landing instructions.

"American planes too?" Chuni asked.

We began to look around. As we neared the Dum Dum Airport, we saw two formations of delta-wing jets streak past us, four in each set. They were U.S. Navy twin-jet attack planes.

Chuni took the hand mike and, during a momentary lapse in transmissions, broke in and asked for landing instructions.

The strong signal of the station at the airport slammed into the receiver, giving her immediate directions.

Another voice interrupted in English.

"American aircraft from carrier Lexington, advised you have primary landing clearance on runway seven dash eight. No more than two aircraft landing at any one time please."

The signal cut off, and the Russian planes were told they would be able to land in approximately seven minutes on runway eight dash zero.

Chuni and I exchanged glances. We didn't have to speak to express the fear that was growing inside us. The two great powers were massing forces in the city.

Friendship visits, they'd call them. Or they'd use some other diplomatic term to justify the invasion of Indian soil now taking place on a small scale. But the results would be tragic if the two powers clashed on neutral ground.

Chuni worked the controls and swept the little Comanche in gracefully, landing on the very start of the strip and moving to the taxi apron at the private air terminal hangars.

My eyebrows had pulled down in concentration. Chuni's questioning glance made me put my thoughts into words.

"This is August fourteenth. Tomorrow is supposed to be the big day. We're so close to a shooting war it makes me sick."

Joe had told me during the flight that although he knew little about the terrorists, he could lead me to their ammunition dump, a place outside the city where they were storing their weapons in preparation for the big attack on the fifteenth.

If we could destroy their munitions, we might be able to block the attack on the consulates and prevent the impending clash between Russia and the United States.

I turned the Mercedes down another street and circled the big stone building the Russians use for their diplomatic work in Calcutta. The shades were drawn. A solid ring of Russian marines lined the sidewalk in front of the building. Each had a rifle over his shoulder and a bandolier of ammunition around his dress uniform. The Russians were ready to fight.

I couldn't see how anyone could get in close enough to throw a bomb, yet I had a hunch the man we were looking for had already made his plans. Somehow he'd get through. But how?

At the U.S. consulate there was a roadblock on each side of the building. U.S. Marines in green fatigue battle uniforms turned back every car.

I took Joe and Chuni with me, and we began working our way through the defenses around the consulate. By the time we got through the big gate and up the steps to the front door, Slocum was coming out to greet us.

"Quite an army you've got," I said. "Isn't the Indian government about to throw you out of the country?"

"The Marines?" Slocum asked. "They're honor guards. We're bringing in planes too . . . just to help the Indians celebrate their Independence Day."

I smirked at the excuse he was using and wondered how New Delhi was reacting. Then Amartya Raj came down the steps.

"The presence of Russian and American forces has my blessing," the Indian police officer said sullenly. "Many governments are sending units to help us mark our independence." He paused and looked deliberately into my eyes. "But subversives have no place in Calcutta, Mr. *Carter.*"

He emphasized my name and formed his lips into a hard, determined line. Slocum gulped and looked guilty.

"I'm sorry," he said to me. "Mr. Raj . . . he found out who you are. He wants to arrest you."

I looked at the big Indian cop and grinned. Defiantly I put out my wrists, ready for the handcuffs.

"Go ahead," I said. "Arrest me."

"There'll be no more trouble," Slocum said with false confidence. "Colonel Woo and the people in New Delhi are working for a reconciliation between us and the Russians."

"We've called in the United States. They'll have an investigative team here within a week."

"A week?"

"Yes." Slocum tried to sound sure of himself and failed. "As long as there are no more terrorist attacks . . ." He let his voice fade away to nothing.

Raj ignored him. He considered me skeptically, then looked at Chuni.

"You have a lead?" he asked. "We should know all the information you have."

"Trust him," Chuni said to the big Indian cop.

Raj scowled but walked ahead of us into Slocum's office. I was surprised to see Alexander Sokoloff sitting there. His rugged face was serious.

"Still alive, Mr. Carter?" he asked.

"Very," I said.

"And the boy . . . who is he?"

"A friend." I said nothing more and Sokoloff

squinted at Joe. The Russian fox sensed the importance of the young Indian but he didn't press for details.

"Mr. Sokoloff came to deliver an ultimatum," Slocum said. "His superiors don't believe we are sincere. They still think we are behind the attacks on their nationals in Calcutta. They think it is part of a larger plan to embarrass them around the world."

"No more," Sokoloff said softly. "No more attacks or we retaliate in force. I have my orders."

He grunted, nodded sharply and left the room. When he was gone, Raj stepped forward. He scowled peevishly and made no attempt to conceal his displeasure.

"I can't let you continue your independent action, Mr. Carter. You are an affront to our national pride. Either you'll confide in me or you'll be restricted to the consulate grounds until this matter is brought to a conclusion."

Chuni stepped between us. She spoke directly to me.

"Take Raj with you," she suggested. "He could help you come out alive."

"Take me where?" Raj asked critically.

I wanted to go to the ammo dump alone, but the Indian cop appeared ready to make that difficult. With less than twenty-four hours left, I didn't have the time to argue.

"All right," I told Raj. "Only no questions. And you come alone. Nobody else. No time to notify your office."

"This is ridiculous," Raj protested. "It could be just a trick to get me away from my headquarters while you continue to harass the Soviets. It could be. . . ."

"Look," I snapped irritably. "As far as I can tell, World War III may be erupting in Calcutta by tomorrow noon. And we may have only one slim chance to prevent it. If you want to help, fine. Otherwise, I'm going alone."

Joe and I were already out the door when the big Indian started after us. He trailed us to the car and rode in silence to my hotel. In my room I dug into the suitcase Hawk had supplied and refitted Wilhelmina with a fresh clip. I found Pierre, the gas pellet, and taped that to my leg, and I tucked a gas-dispensing fountain pen in my breast pocket.

I changed shirts and switched handkerchiefs, making sure to pick the big, fancy linen ones that Hawk insists on including whenever anyone at headquarters does my packing.

I offered Raj some special weapons, but he shook his head. He was content with the heavily chromed .45 on his hip.

The sun was setting behind the buildings in the west by the time we had climbed into the Mercedes, and I had begun to follow Joe's directions.

An hour later we were still cruising the outskirts of Calcutta as Joe tried to recall where Zakir had met him. Finally, he motioned me to the side of the road and jumped out as soon as the car came to a stop.

"Yes," he said confidently. "Around here someplace."

He made a motion with his arm, pointing across the rice paddies that pressed in on the edges of the city.

We started across the fields, but Amartya Raj hesitated, cursing quietly to himself, calling himself a fool for going with us. Only when I started to move faster did he follow. Together we walked steadily south until we came to a stone wall.

"This is the place," Joe said.

Raj came forward and looked at the wall critically. He said he could see nothing sinister in the age-old stone. I stopped his hand inches from a trip wire that ran along the top. The wire extended through screw eyes an inch above the fence. It was set to react with either an upward or downward pressure.

Raj said nothing, but the wire surprised him. It wasn't the kind of thing you saw along the wall of a peasant's farm; it was a warning device you'd expect to see in combat.

Joe went first, with a leg up from me. He stepped carefully over the wire and jumped softly to the ground. I helped Raj over next and followed him.

Joe motioned from a dozen feet ahead. I moved up. The land inside the fence had been leveled into pastures, and the rice paddy dikes had long since broken down. In the soft moonlight I saw only grassland and small rows of trees.

We moved down the side of the fence, using the trees for cover. Every two hundred yards we stopped and listened.

Even so, we almost missed the first guard. He was

leaning against a tree and looking away from us, listening to a transistor radio. We went around him.

The moon slid behind the clouds as we moved to the open pasture, running quietly, checking a quarter-mile-wide swath, but not sure what we were looking for.

A faint whiff of smoke caught my attention. Another gust of wind brought the unmistakable smell of cheap cigarette smoke. We saw a small red glow ahead to the left, about three hundred yards away.

Soon we spotted a guard in a makeshift uniform. His presence was enough to assure us that we were on the right track. Even Raj bent lower and moved more carefully as we circled past the man.

A mile past the woods we came to a favorable sign, a road running along a row of trees.

"Yes, we came this way in a truck," Joe said, excitement shining in his eyes.

A hundred yards ahead I saw a long, low storage building. The top was completely covered with sod and bushes and the ends sloped down so the structure would be impossible to spot from the air.

We circled the building carefully. Ahead were more trees. The road ended, but as we worked into the woods, we found a small path that had been hacked through the brush. We followed it and soon came to a covered parking area. Under it were several Indian army jeeps, all of them surprisingly new. How had they come to be here in a camp I assumed to be run by the terrorists?

"What's wrong?" Raj asked sharply. "Why are we waiting?"

"The jeeps . . . stolen from the army, I suppose."

Raj answered, "Yes. Or sold to the terrorists. There is corruption everywhere."

Joe tugged at my sleeve, then jointed farther ahead. "Up there," he said anxiously. "The ammo dump."

I searched the area he indicated and saw lights sparkling in front of the trees.

Halfway to the big lights we came to a low stone building. It was in the open with no camouflage and I could see it had been there a long time. A road ran directly up to the building and stopped at a big drive-in door.

Joe and I started to move forward but Raj whispered an objection.

"We had better go back," he said.

"Why?"

"For reinforcements. I can muster a hundred men . . . a thousand if we need them. We'll surround the buildings. We'll arrest everyone inside."

He stood up but I pulled him back down beside me.

"They'll be gone before we return," I said.

"But we can't go in there alone," he snapped. "We wouldn't have a chance."

"You got a better idea?"

"It's illegal," the big cop argued.

I wanted to laugh. Instead, I motioned to Joe and we moved closer to the building.

A guard with an automatic rifle was walking almost

directly toward us. A second later and he would have spotted us, but Joe reacted almost instinctively. He stood up boldly and spoke in Hindi a pleasant greeting that distracted the guard.

The man brought his gun into position, but it was too late. I was on him. And this time I had exactly what I needed . . . Pierre, the little gas pellet I keep between my legs.

I released it in the man's face and watched the startled expression form as he breathed in deeply before he realized what was happening.

He was dead when I let him slip to the ground.

It took only thirty seconds to open the lock on the door, and then we were inside.

A dozen cases of grenades were stacked along one wall, all marked with the Indian army imprint. Along the other wall were boxes of rifles, some open, others still nailed shut. There were even a few mortar and shoulder-held artillery pieces toward the rear, enough to equip a small band of guerrillas. But mainly the building was filled with homemade bombs—the two-rupee wonders that had been used to pit the Americans and Russians against each other in the past few days.

I was still admiring the cache of weapons when a guard appeared in the doorway at the far end of the long, narrow building.

There had been no warning—I hadn't seen or heard him. He just seemed to come out of the shadows, his automatic weapon held at his hip.

He was thin and young, hardly into his twenties, wearing the makeshift uniform I had seen on some of the troops in the village. He didn't hesitate; he aimed and fired.

He chose Joe first and the kid didn't have a chance. The slugs caught him in the belly and flung him backward. He was dead before he hit the dirt floor of the building.

The next two seconds seemed to last an eternity. My hand was digging for Wilhelmina, my legs bending, dropping me to the floor; and my eyes were fixed on the guard's chest. I already had the point picked out where I was going to shoot him if I lived long enough. In the chest, between his windpipe and his heart.

I didn't expect to make it. The automatic rifle was swinging fast, away from Joe's bloodied body and straight toward Amartya Raj. A couple of slugs for the big cop and the rest for me; that was all the guard had to do.

As I rolled I caught a glimpse of Raj's face. It was rigid, but there was no fear. He seemed to be waiting to be killed. His hands were still at his side.

I was on the floor, rolling for cover, when the guard's automatic weapon leveled on Raj's belly.

But the guard didn't fire. For the time it takes to wink, the gun aimed squarely at the big cop.

When Raj didn't move, the guard whirled, continuing his swing. But his momentum had been broken, and that gave me a chance to roll behind a stack of crates. The guard hesitated, afraid of shooting into the explosives around me.

I trusted my weapon. I fired twice; both slugs hit him in the chest. He screamed once before he hit the floor.

When it was over, I came from behind the crates cautiously. Raj still stood in the center of the access aisle that led through the stacks of ammunition.

We stared at each other, neither of us moving. Then I swung my gun toward him. He didn't seem surprised.

"Put your forty-five on the floor," I told him.

He smirked at me.

"You are giving the orders now, Mr. Carter?" he sneered.

"You're one of them," I accused him.

I was only guessing, but I couldn't forget that brief second when the guard seemed to recognize the big cop and let him live.

"You're forgetting," Raj said. "I'm a high-ranking official in the government. You think anyone will believe you?" He smiled confidently when I didn't answer.

He tipped his head and listened to a sound in the distance.

I heard it too—a truck changing gears as it climbed a small hill.

"My men," he explained. "They've come for their weapons."

"For tomorrow?"

"Yes."

"But what do you hope to accomplish?"

"We'll overthrow the state rule. We can create enough confusion so that the central government in New Delhi will order martial law. They've done it before. Only this time we'll see to it that there's no official left alive to take control."

"Except you."

"Yes."

"Bull," I said. I waved my pistol at the arms around us. "You haven't got enough supplies or men to take over the city, let alone the entire state."

He shrugged. "We're willing to take the chance."

"We?" I asked.

"I've told you enough," he said.

He looked back over his shoulder toward the door we had entered. From outside we could hear the truck coming to a stop and the sound of men piling out. They were in good spirits, talking and laughing as men do sometimes before they go into combat. When the first one reached the door and saw Raj, he smiled in recognition. His expression changed, though, when he saw the gun in my hand.

Raj spoke to him sharply in Hindi, and the man backed away from the door. Outside there was a great deal of shouting and movement; then suddenly everything was silent.

Amartya Raj sneered at me again. "Well, Mr. Carter, what do you do now? You're surrounded. And you're standing in the middle of several tons of explosives."

"If I die, you die," I said quietly.

He shrugged. "I'm a Hindu. I doubt that death holds quite the same terror for me as it does for you. So, I repeat, Mr. Carter, exactly what are you going to do? Give me your gun or wait for my men to blow us both to a million pieces?"

CHAPTER XIII

In poker when your last dollar is on the table, you might as well bluff.

So as I stood in that warehouse with a truckload of armed men outside and tons of explosives inside, I decided to gamble. There was only one way out, and that required Raj as an escort. He'd have to call off his troops if I hoped to get out of there alive. But even a Luger muzzle at his head didn't seem to faze him.

Raj was a pro, a trained expert in weapons and explosives, just like me. But I had one advantage, my reputation. So I laid it on the table and hoped.

"Give me your gun and your watch," I said.

"My what?"

He hesitated, and I tapped him on the side of his head with the Luger. He slumped to the floor and I stripped the watch and the forty-five from him.

When he regained consciousness, I was just finishing my little contraption.

It was a Rube Goldberg design if I ever saw one, but it looked as if it would work.

The heart of the whole thing was a grenade. I had pulled the pin and then reinserted it just enough to barely hold the safety handle in place. Then I knocked the crystal from Raj's watch and broke off the second hand before I balanced a pencil on the face.

I tried to make it look like the minute hand of the watch would knock over the pencil. And the falling pencil would knock the precariously positioned pin from the grenade. If it did, we'd have four seconds to run.

When I showed it to Raj, he laughed. "You can't be serious. That'll never work."

I looked surprised. "Oh? Why not? It worked in Hong Kong. Maybe you heard about it. I used it as a booby trap for an old Chinese smuggler. Blew his head off, right on schedule."

"Well, sure," Raj conceded. "Maybe once. If the pin were just barely inserted . . . if the pencil were heavy enough . . . if the watch were tightly wound . . . if. . . ."

I wanted to laugh. In spite of himself, he was backing away. I moved with him. Ten feet, twenty feet, we kept moving back, our eyes on the ridiculous-looking contraption. It sat on top of an open box filled with mortar shells. If the grenade blew, so would the shells and everything in the building. It would be quite a display.

"Of course, we could run," I said.

"What?" His gaze didn't leave the grenade.

"Together," I said. "We could run for the truck.

Lock step . . . me right behind you. You'd yell at your men as we ran. You'd tell them not to shoot."

"Go to hell," he said.

We had backed as far away from the contraption as we could. We stood just inside the door. I could hear his men shouting at us from outside. They were waiting for his orders.

"Take your time," I told him calmly. "I mean, you've got ninety seconds."

He stared at me briefly, then looked at the grenade. "Seventy seconds," I said. "Plenty of time. Of course, you don't care . . . being a Hindu and all." I glanced at my watch. "Sixty seconds."

He was starting to sweat. So was I.

"It might work," he mumbled. "It just might work."

"Forty-five seconds."

Now I was looking at the thing. I swore I could hear it ticking.

"You don't suppose it'll work, do you?" I asked myself. "You don't suppose. . . ."

I couldn't even finish the sentence in my head. Suddenly it wasn't funny.

"Thirty-two seconds . . . thirty-one."

I wasn't counting for Raj anymore. I was counting for myself.

"Dammit, Carter," the big cop shouted. "Stop that fool thing. In the name of all that's holy." Unwillingly I stepped toward it. His hand grabbed my arm, stopping me. "No, don't," he cried. "You might jar it. You might. . . ."

I looked at my watch. "My God, ten seconds . . . nine . . . eight."

"Run!" he yelled. "Hurry!"

We didn't think. We ran. Straight out the door.

I heard him yelling in Hindi and I was right behind him, the gun square in his back. I couldn't understand what he was saying. I could only hope he was ordering his men to hold their fire.

I saw his troops; some of them had guns aimed at us. He must have shouted something else, too, because suddenly the armed men broke positions and scattered. They were fleeing right behind us.

We had reached the truck when Raj whirled and whipped at me with his muscular arm. He caught me on the chin, staggering me momentarily.

I fired the Luger and missed.

Somebody behind me also fired, and I leaped for the truck. I tried two more quick shots at Raj, but I couldn't see if I hit him.

Then the ammo dump went. Either my contraption worked, or a stray slug set it off. I'll never know, but the low-lying building erupted like a Fourth of July finale. The first flash was a blinding gush of light that left white spots in my vision. Next came the roar, a fist of sound driven against the ears. Then the heat that slapped at my face and pressure that shoved me against the truck.

Shells and grenades tossed into the air by the original explosion popped when they hit the ground. Rifle bullets cracked in a deadly staccato as debris slashed through the air around me.

I saw one man thrown into the air, his body twisted and torn before it landed. Others died instantly or staggered around in circles through the hail of shells until something ignited close enough to cut them in half.

I got the truck started and drove straight across the dried rice paddies toward the Mercedes. The explosions were still lighting the night sky behind me when I slipped into the car.

I didn't know if anyone was still alive back at the rebels' ammo dump, and I was too stunned to care.

I had driven nearly a mile before I realized my left arm was limp. My shoulder ached and when I put my hand up to check it, I could feel the shrapnel sticking through the cloth of my jacket.

I was afraid I didn't have much time before I would lose consciousness, and I had a gnawing suspicion that the problem wasn't finished yet. I had wiped out the terrorists' supplies, perhaps even killed most of their key men, but I wasn't satisfied. There was still one small aspect I wanted to check out.

So I needed help, someone to keep me on my feet until the crisis was past.

There was only one place I could go. And I hoped I would get there before I passed out.

Chuni's cool hands gently spread the tape across the

hole in my shoulder. Then she leaned down and kissed me where it hurt.

Instinctively I rolled over and tried to take her in my arms, but the pain was still too intense.

"Poor darling," she said. "Lucky you weren't killed."

I sat up, trying to orient myself.

I was in her apartment on the bed where we had made love so recently.

"You wrecked the Mercedes," she added. "You passed out as you came into the drive."

She walked away from the bed and went to the window. When she threw back the drapes, the sun glared in.

"My God!" I gasped. "It's morning."

"You slept all night. You needed it."

I reached for my clothes and she ran to me, trying to push me back.

"You don't understand," I said. "It's the fifteenth . . . the big attack . . . it may come today. We've got to stop it."

She laughed gently and laid a hand on my brow. "Don't you remember? You solved all that."

"What?"

"The terrorists' supply dump . . . you destroyed it last night. You and Raj."

I scowled at her curiously. "You heard about that?"

"Of course. The whole city has. I could hear the explosions even from here."

My brain felt fuzzy. I couldn't quite comprehend what she was saying until she mentioned Raj again.

"Amartya told me everything."

"Raj? He's alive?"

"Yes, hurt but alive. He wants you at the ceremonies today at the government house."

I cursed to myself. The bastard was still living.

"He's sending a car for you," she said. "An escort."

Suddenly I understood. I knew too much. Raj was sending an escort for me all right—a couple of hatchet men, no doubt, who would make certain I never talked again.

"When?"

"Soon. Any minute."

I pushed her aside and walked to the window. In the courtyard below I could see a car turning into the drive. Chuni protested, but I dressed hurriedly, trying to explain as I did.

We escaped the apartment just ahead of the two men from the car in the courtyard. They were being escorted up to Chuni's bedroom by the maid as we slipped out the back way.

"Ridiculous," Chuni argued as we climbed into her cream-colored Bentley. "Raj couldn't be involved with the terrorists. He wouldn't send men to kill you. I know him."

But even as she said it, a 45-caliber hole opened in the hood of her car. Another appeared in the fender as I swerved the Bentley along the drive to the gate.

When we reached the street, she could see the men in the window of her bedroom where they had gone to search for us. The guns in their hands were still spitting slugs in our direction.

"It's true," she said. "Then Raj is the leader of the terrorists . . . the man in back of the bombings?"

"No," I said. My own answer surprised me. I suddenly felt Raj wasn't the top man among the terrorists, not the brain behind the entire plot, although I had no real reasons—just things he had said or maybe the loose ends that still troubled me about the assignment.

"Then who is?" Chuni asked.

I didn't know. Although we had already put too much distance between us and the house to fear the men Raj had sent to kill me, I kept my foot heavy on the accelerator. My eyes stayed on my watch. I had a gnawing fear that half the town was going to blow up any minute.

Chuni tried to calm me. "Slow down," she begged. "There's no rush now. Raj can't go through with the plot," she argued. "You destroyed their supplies. You killed most of their men. He can't expect to go through with their plans."

What she said made sense, but I still couldn't relax. Too many questions still haunted me. Then suddenly I thought I knew where I would get the answers.

I said nothing to Chuni as I turned the Bentley onto a major thoroughfare and cut south toward the consulate. Already the street had taken on a festive appearance with flags draped from every lamppost. The sidewalks were beginning to fill with people in holiday garb moving toward the government buildings in the heart of Calcutta.

"They are going to see the ceremonies," Chuni explained.

"When?" I asked anxiously.

"At noon."

I glanced at my watch. It was eleven-thirty.

The deeper we got into the city, the thicker the crowds, until we were moving at a snail's pace. The people were colorful in their native dress. They shouted to us good-naturedly, but the sight of their numbers appalled me. I kept seeing them not as people but as grains of powder ready to ignite at the touch of a match.

The situation in front of the American consulate didn't relieve my anxiety either. The American troops were still there. They carried their weapons and their belts were heavy with loaded clips of ammunition, but they wore dress blues, and the people mingled among them.

They had let down their guard completely.

"They know the terrorists have been wiped out," Chuni explained as we rolled through the gate into the front yard of the consulate. "So do the Russians."

I groaned, but she laughed and called me an alarmist.

"It's over," she said confidently. "There'll be no trouble. Later we'll have Amartya arrested. He can do nothing alone."

I didn't argue. I just leaped out of the car and raced into the consulate.

Slocum was coming down the stairs as I entered. Gone was the fear from his eyes and the sweat from his forehead. He was the calm, cool, career diplomat again. He scowled when he saw me, and I knew it was because I reminded him of how he had almost cracked these last few days when he thought the world was going to start tearing itself apart right in his domain.

"Oh, Mr. Carter," he said without smiling. "Are you going to the ceremonies?"

I shouted at him. "The troops outside . . . they're not keeping the people back."

He sneered at me condescendingly. "That's over now. Mr. Raj's people wiped out the terrorists last night. I believe you helped."

"There could still be an attack," I insisted. "A single bomb thrown at the Russian consulate and they'd come out shooting."

"Relax, Mr. Carter," Slocum said. "The matter is now in the hands of professionals . . . the diplomats. And we have the situation under control."

He placed a hand comfortingly on my shoulder, treating me like a child. "In fact, we're extending a hand of friendship to the Russians this very morning." He raised his watch and checked it. "In ten minutes, to be exact. Their Mr. Sokoloff will be greeting our little delegation. I'll have to hurry to be there."

"Delegation?" I asked.

He brushed past me. His chauffeur, a Marine in full uniform, held open the door and Slocum started out to the car in front of the building.

"Colonel Woo's idea," he called.

He had reached the car when I grabbed his shoulder.

"Wait," I snapped at him. "What's this about Colonel Woo?"

Irritably he knocked my hand away. "Look, Carter, your job's done here. You did your work—a bloody, gory job, I might add. So get out of Calcutta while you still can."

He turned back to the car, but I grabbed him again and pushed him hard against the door.

The Marine chauffeur took a step toward me, then stopped.

"Damn you, Slocum," I growled. "Answer me. What's this about Colonel Woo?"

"None of your concern," he said, "but we had a brilliant idea. A peace gesture. Children bearing flowers to the Russian consulate. It'll be on television worldwide by satellite."

I dropped my hand from his coat. I couldn't believe what he had said. "Children," I said.

"Yes, from Colonel Woo's orphange. Hundreds of them. Carrying flowers from us to the Russians. Brilliant, isn't it?"

"No . . ." I stepped back from him, realizing he had never really known how the terrorists had worked.

Slocum turned away from me and swung into the

car, closing the door after him. Just then Chuni joined me.

"He said there'd be children, didn't he?" she whispered. "Then that's how . . ." She stopped, the thought not quite formed in her mind. "I mean, it isn't over. Not yet. And Colonel Woo . . ."

"Yes," I said. "It must be Colonel Woo. But they'll blame the Americans. Slocum . . . that fool . . . he's played right into Woo's hands." I started back for the Bentley, and Chuni came after me.

"What are you going to do?" she cried.

"Stop it if I can." I slid in beside the wheel as she ran to the other door. "No, I'm going alone," I told her. "It could be dangerous."

She ignored me and got in the car.

"If it was Colonel Woo, why did he give us the information about Zakir and the temple?" Chuni asked.

"Zakir was compromised. We knew his name, so he had to be destroyed. Woo must have hoped to have us killed at the same time. It almost worked."

I leaned on the horn and raced out of the consulate gate. A Marine guard jumped clear and cursed me in voice loud enough to be heard halfway up the block.

Ahead of us the people scrambled for the sidewalks. A police officer shouted at us and waved his hands frantically, but I didn't slow until we approached the Russian consulate.

For a moment I thought I had panicked unnecessarily. Like the Americans, the Russians had relaxed their guard. Their troops, also in dress uniform, appeared more ceremonial than military. But then I felt a sinking sensation as I spotted the contingent of American Marines at stark attention in formation across the street from the consulate. Slocum had put a hair trigger on the situation by bringing a platoon of Marines with him.

His car was just ahead of ours and, as I swerved the Bentley to the curb, his chauffeur was just pulling through the gate into the fenced enclosure. I could see Alexander Sokoloff, too, coming out the main entrance of the building, ready to meet his guests.

"Look!" Chuni shouted. She pointed frantically up the street.

They were coming over a slight rise, a hundred of them at least. Children, most not into their teens. A small army of them, all singing . . . all headed toward the Russian consulate. All carrying small bouquets of flowers set in brightly painted tin cans.

Slocum climbed out of his car, beaming proudly and looking toward the children as if they were a personal diplomatic triumph. Even the old fox Sokoloff appeared pleased.

"Stop them," I yelled.

I felt like an idiot. I ran up the street shouting, Chuni right behind me.

I could hear Slocum crying out to me. The people along the street stared at me as if I were a madman.

A cop came out to block my path; I knocked him aside and charged into the children.

I saw Colonel Woo then. He was off to the side, watching but leaving the leadership up to a teen-age boy from his orphanage.

Everything happened fast. The children were stunned by the sight of a tall white man charging into their midst. They stopped singing and fell back.

The cop was still trying to get to me, and some of the people in the street were crowding in too. Frantically I started grabbing the bouquets from the children's hands. I checked one, found nothing and threw it aside. Then I checked another and another.

The children were screaming around me. Some were running back the way they had come. I found nothing until Chuni cried out to me and handed me a small tin can topped with flowers. I flung the blooms aside and held up the bomb beneath it.

Just as I had suspected.

Woo had even wangled the American consulate staff into taking the blame since, as far as the Russians knew, it was Slocum who had arranged the children's march on their consulate. When the bombs started to fly, the Russian reaction would be explosive.

But I had no time to explain all that. The police were closing in on me. So were some of the people from the street. I could even see the Marine platoon breaking ranks and moving in my direction.

I took a wild chance. I whipped out my lighter and lit the short fuse that protruded from the top of the can.

A gasp spread through the crowd. People fell back,

knocking each other to the ground in their rush to escape. I whirled, looking for a place to throw the bomb, but there were people almost everywhere.

Finally I saw Colonel Woo. He stood alone, back near the glass entrance of a modern office building. At least it was away from the Russian consulate. Hopefully, Sokoloff would understand I was trying to prevent an attack on his staff.

I heaved the small bomb like a grenade. It hit the concrete in front of Woo and rolled.

He had backed into the building before it went off, but the plate glass window shattered and sprayed him with fragments. I saw him go down; then lost sight of him.

Around me the crowd was running. The children had dropped their bouquets and were crying.

I ran toward the building where I had seen Woo. Inside my feet crunched on broken glass, and I could see the trail of blood leading from the point where Colonel Woo had fallen.

Ahead of me the doors of an elevator were closing.

I flung myself at the narrowing gap between the sliding doors.

I made it, but it almost cost me my life.

CHAPTER XIV

The second I landed inside the elevator the colonel fell on me. He moved fast. His hands were all over me, searching for a weapon. I thrust my hands to cover Wilhelmina and the knife, but I felt him snatch something from the pocket of my jacket.

"Don't move," he shouted.

He had climbed off me now and stood above me. "Turn slowly," he ordered.

Ever so carefully I looked back over my shoulder. He leaned against the closed door, one hand ready to push the controls that would start us on the long run to the top floor of the building.

His face was cut to ribbons. Slivers of glass still protruded from some of the slices. Blood poured from his chest, and there was one long slash across his abdomen that looked like it should have killed him, yet there was a certain dignity about him even now. With death only minutes away, he maintained the precise, dapper touch that had impressed me at his estate.

In his hand he held my fountain pen, the one loaded with deadly gas. He had already flipped open the top and his finger was on the clip, ready to fire. Obviously he knew how it worked.

He aimed it at me, and I wondered if he realized its full strength.

"Use that in here," I warned, "and you'll die with me."

"One breath," he said. "That's all it takes. I know the device well, Mr. Carter."

I thought I saw his finger move and I almost shouted at him.

"Wait," I said. "There's no hurry."

He laughed and motioned for me to rise. Carefully I got to my feet, keeping the width of the car between us.

"Just tell me why," I said. "What were you trying to achieve?"

"Power, Mr. Carter," he explained. "You asked me what more a man like me could want. I told you a man who has everything wants only security."

"And you lied?"

"No, but I failed to explain. Only power provides security. Only the man on top is safe."

"I still don't understand. What did you hope to accomplish with the bombs?"

"Chaos," he said. "The Russians would have blamed the Americans. There would have been shooting. Riots in the street. A small war, right here in Calcutta. New Delhi would have declared martial law, as they have before. Raj would have taken control. Later we would have declared independence for the state of Bengal."

"But he worked for you?"

"Yes."

"A front man because you're Chinese?"

He nodded again and began to double over with pain.

"You're dying," I warned him. "He'll have control now without you."

He shook his head weakly. "There are documents. They'll be opened after my death."

"Implicating Raj in the plot?"

"Yes."

He stiffened his back and raised the gas gun a little higher.

"But you failed," I said. "You die for nothing."

He pushed the control button behind him. Gently the elevator started to rise.

He breathed deeply then and pressed the clip on the fountain pen. I gasped for breath just before the gas squirted out between us.

It filled the small compartment, swirling around us like a tiger, ready to pounce the second we opened our mouths to gasp for air.

We stood there, staring at each other in a deadly, silent contest, holding our breaths. Neither of us moved. There was no escape. The slow-moving elevator was on a run to the top floor. I couldn't fight my may past him in time to make an intermediate stop. I would have to breathe before I could open the door.

He was smirking, self-satisfied. Death would be easier for him now. He would go to his grave thinking he had won the final contest. This was better than outshooting me at the trap range. If he could hold his breath just a second longer than I could, he would have his final triumph.

I reached in my pocket and pulled out my handkerchief, the special one Hawk always insists I carry when I take the gas gun on an assignment.

I placed it across my mouth and nose, then breathed comfortably through the special filtering fibers.

First confusion, then understanding, then horror showed on Woo's face. He reddened; he even cupped his hands over his mouth. But in the end he had to breathe. He exhaled and leaped toward me, his small hands grabbing for my throat. I didn't fight back.

Even as his fingers tightened on my neck, he breathed in. "Damn you," he cried. Our eyes met for a moment.

Then his fingers slowly relaxed and slipped away.

He was dead when he hit the floor.

I let the gas dissipate on the upper floor and started the slow ride down. When the elevator door opened again on the main floor of the building, Chuni ran to me.

Outside in the building lobby a crowd of bewildered people watched.

Slocum was there, his face moist again with perspiration. He glowered at me, humiliated. I ignored him and turned instead to Alexander Sokoloff, who came forward from the crowd.

The Russian smiled pleasantly. He even leaned forward to kiss me on each cheek, as his countrymen like to do with their comrades.

"You saved us all," he said as his lips brushed past my ear. "But leave Calcutta tonight," he whispered.

Then he was stepping back, smiling, making diplomatic noises about Americans and Russians living in peace everywhere, even Calcutta.

Behind him I saw Amartya Raj, his left arm in a cast, his face bruised from the explosion at the munitions dump. He held himself erect, but I guessed at the terror inside him. Sooner or later he would be exposed. It was only a matter of time.

Finally, Chuni's hand was in mine and she was leading me out to the Bentley.

"My place or yours?" she asked.

I looked back into the building and thought of what Sokoloff had said.

I ought to keep moving. By morning his men would try to kill me. Even before that, Raj might send out his cutthroats. Calcutta was a dangerous place; but then I looked at Chuni and remembered.

"Your place," I said. "The bed is softer."

AWARD

NICK CARTER

Don't Miss a Single
Killmaster Spy Chiller

SAIGON　　　　　　　　　　　　　Nick Carter
A cauldron where each caress can lead to sudden mayhem.　　　　　　　　　　　　AX0625—60¢

AMSTERDAM　　　　　　　　　　　Nick Carter
A wanton blonde is the only lead to a private spy network.　　　　　　　　　　　AX0628—60¢

TEMPLE OF FEAR　　　　　　　　　Nick Carter
N3 assumes the identity of a man long dead.
　　　　　　　　　　　　　　　　　AX0629—60¢

MISSION TO VENICE　　　　　　　Nick Carter
A missing H-bomb triggers a game of global blackmail.
　　　　　　　　　　　　　　　　　AX0632—60¢

A KOREAN TIGER　　　　　　　　Nick Carter
N3 must recover stolen nuclear plans that can crush America to dust.　　　　　　　　AX0634—60¢

THE MIND POISONERS　　　　　　Nick Carter
A vicious international plot hooks American college kids on a violence drug.　　　　　AX0636—60¢

THE CHINA DOLL　　　　　　　　Nick Carter
Nick Carter is the first white man in the "Forbidden City" of Peking.　　　　　　AX0638—60¢

CHECKMATE IN RIO　　　　　　　Nick Carter
Sex and savagery are the facts of life for every agent.
　　　　　　　　　　　　　　　　　AX0639—60¢

THE RED GUARD Nick Carter
Peking was ready to unleash a super-bomb—more
lethal than any America or Russia had ever built. It
was Nick Carter's job to destroy it! AN1089—95¢

JEWEL OF DOOM Nick Carter
Hidden inside the most heavily guarded ruby on earth
is a nuclear secret America needs desperately. Nick
Carter's assignment: steal the jewel! AN1090—95¢

MOSCOW Nick Carter
American Intelligence sends Nick inside the Kremlin
to ferret out and destroy a new super-weapon. His
contact: a beautiful Soviet double agent . . .
AN1091—95¢

TIME CLOCK OF DEATH Nick Carter
The Soviets' super-spy jet had been hijacked, and
the Kremlin blamed America. Nick Carter's mission:
find the jet before the Russians attack! AN1092—95¢

THE MIND KILLERS Nick Carter
They were all-American heroes—scientifically program-
med to assassinate. Nick Carter's orders: stop them
before they reach the President of the United States!
AN1093—95¢

THE WEAPON OF NIGHT Nick Carter
Total annihilation threatens under cover of paralysing
power failures. AN1094—95¢

ISTANBUL Nick Carter
America's super-spy finds sultry love and sudden violence in the Middle East. AN1095—95¢

SEVEN AGAINST GREECE Nick Carter
A death duel with Princess Electra, whose evil beauty
N3 can't resist. AN1096—95¢

RHODESIA Nick Carter
A revenge-crazed Nazi brings the Middle East to the
edge of disaster. AN1097—95¢

THE MARK OF COSA NOSTRA Nick Carter
A grisly Mafia manhunt—an assignment exploding
with sex, savagery, and revenge. AN1098—95¢

SECRET MISSION

*"...the best new
adventure and intrigue series
to come along in years"*
(Archer Winston, The New York *Post*)
